THE DEAD BLUE SEA

COREY PHILLIPS

This is a work of fiction. Names, characters, places, dialogue, and incidents either are the product of the author's imagination or are used fictitiously. Any resemblance to actual persons, living or dead, events, or locales is entirely coincidental.

Copyright © 2023, Corey Phillips.

All rights reserved. No part of this publication may be reproduced, distributed, or transmitted in any form or by any means, including photocopying, recording, or other electronic or mechanical methods, without the prior written permission of the publisher and/or author, except in the case of brief quotations embodied in critical reviews and certain other noncommercial uses permitted by copyright law.

ISBN: 978-1-7373608-6-5 (Paperback)

Book Cover/Page Illustrations copyright © 2023, by Corey Phillips

First print edition 2023.

Published under American Backroad Publishing, LLC, Saltville, VA.

Printed in the United States of America.

Other works by the Author

2021

THE PARSONAGE
2022

www.americanbackroadpublishing.com

Table of Contents

CHAPTER 1 - THE SEA HELLION 1

CHAPTER 2 - COMANCHE 14

CHAPTER 3 - STOWAWAYS 24

CHAPTER 4 - SHIPPING OUT 35

CHAPTER 5 - INITIATION 48

CHAPTER 6 - WAYFARING STRANGER 61

CHAPTER 7 - THE GRAND BANKS 73

CHAPTER 8 - THE MULE 89

CHAPTER 9 - ST. ELMO 106

CHAPTER 10 - SHRAPNEL 118

CHAPTER 11 - THE SEA WHISPERS 127

CHAPTER 12 - BLOOD MONEY 140

CHAPTER 13 - PARANOIA 157

CHAPTER 14 - THE MUTINY 171

CHAPTER 15 - TAKING THE SHIP 182

CHAPTER 16 - ADRIFT 194

CHAPTER 17 - THE DAMNED 207

CHAPTER 18 - MAKE CHASE 218

CHAPTER 19 - A STORM OF FIRE 230

CHAPTER 20 - ABANDON SHIP 245

CHAPTER 21 - THE PHANTOM SHIP 257

CHAPTER 22 - OUT OF THE FOG 272

CHAPTER 23 - GOING AHAB 281

Chapter 1 - The Sea Hellion

She is the deadliest type of beautiful to me. A true temptress in every sense that can claim the lowly. Here with her is a place to find passion and cruelty. She covets and hates, loves and lives with many, but I have still missed her so. When I see a glimpse of her through the windows, for the first time in what feels like a lifetime ago, I am somehow set at ease. The skies have turned her gray with the nearing winter season, but I will return to her. Nothing else makes sense anymore, except only to heed her call. Those waves that come in, they whisper to all nearby who are willing to listen to her. She is the sea.

A return to unwanted conflicts in foreign waters may be suitable enough to mend this desire. But instead, I choose to return to her here at this place, time and time again. The greyhound tires slow down to a screeching stop and the diesel engine shuts off. The bus driver rushes to unload the luggage from under the bus. It takes a few steps to get my bearings again, but I grab my single duffle and throw it over my back. Others look for their mounds of luggage, tourists and more travelers that have been on the same bus with me for the better part of two days. The typical sights here may disappoint, unless they're the type of visitor heavy into the history books. The Fisherman's Memorial was as far as the bus would take us. Camera flashes for photos and selfies are taken by the statue before most of them move on.

I remember playing on the beach side near this statue. My school friends and I would pose next to it as if we were all on a boat full of salty fishermen. I can picture me and my band of grade school buddies now while looking up at the statue of the strong and fearless sailor. Some days we were pirates and some days we were battleship commanders. But at the end of some seasons, a new cluster of names would be added to the memorial inside and we would dread the day to come if we ourselves would ever be added to that same wall; or wonder if they would place a new brick right below the statue for one of us.

I prop up next to the statue and sit on my duffle to look out at the open ocean. My instrument case leaves a bulge inside my duffle but is strong enough to hold my weight without crushing it. My phone gets pulled out to find no new text messages, only a single missed call with a voicemail is all I am worth to her. In a wishful thought, I guess I hoped a sudden cluster of texts would appear in my hands just by pulling the phone out of my pocket. She stayed behind in servitude, while I knew I just couldn't do it anymore. No *"I miss you"* or fake apologies, not even a *"Where did you go?"* from her. Just nothing but a single voicemail from her. So, I was likely never anything to her during our time together. She has a new ranking officer to love up on now until she tires of him too.

But none of that matters anymore. Now, I stand before my first love. I delete the voicemail, turn off the phone, and throw it down on the rocks below to shatter into oblivion. I try to rub the green dinge off the copper St. Peter that mom gave me before I left for the Navy. She had the Fisherman's Prayer engraved on the back. It's all she really had to offer before I left, but I don't hate her for it.

This town has barely changed since I left. Everything just seems smaller somehow. The old buildings and fish markets are still in place, just more worn down. A few chain fast-food joints have come in for the tourists, but most locals still resort to the old pubs and grills that have been here longer than I can remember. My parents met at one before my sister and I were born. Mom was a bartender and Dad was a tourist-based charter boat captain back then. Even after they split up when I was just a teenager, my sister worked at that same bar with mom. I decide to stop by the old pub first to catch any familiar faces and maybe a shot or two to calm my nerves from the long trip.

The after-work crowd is shuffling in and I get blasted with the smell of fish covered dock workers the moment I walk in the door. The smoke fills the dimly lit room, but there's just enough glare coming from all the TVs to reveal a cheering crowd for a game-day that I was unaware of. A distasteful looking grunge band strumming instruments in the corner quietly, with the possibility of knowing their gig is pointless when a football game is on. I sit away from the TVs and the commotion of grumbling geezers by the bar.

"Isaac… Is that you?" a familiar face asks. The barkeep walks over to get a better look at me as I smile back in return.

"Donavan. How are you, man?" I stand up from my booth to shake his hand. He goes to wipe his palms off on his stained apron before reaching back out, but resorts to rubbing them on the white shirt on top of his enormous belly that hangs underneath.

"Oh my God. It is you. I thought I saw you walk in. Hey guys, it's Isaac!" he says while turning around to the patrons that give a faint cheer and briefly raise their mugs. "Wait a sec. Let me get you a drink. Are ya hungry or anything?"

"No thanks, Don. I'll just take whatever's best on tap these days and a shot of Jameson."

"Sure thing, kid. I'll get myself one too. Be right back."

He hobbles away with his aging legs and returns with two shot glasses and a beer. We both settle back into the booth. The floors under his weight groan and the bench seat stresses just as much.

"Here's to you. Welcome home, Isaac." He raises his glass with a smile. We tap the shot glasses and guzzle them down. Some of his whiskey drizzles down from his short beard. We slam them down and he just keeps smiling at me. "How long you been back? We haven't seen you around here since… Well, ya know."

"Yeah… My mom's funeral. I know."

"We really miss ya around here, kid. Your mom too. She worked this bar for a long time. We'd be hoppin' every night after them docks closed down. You were just a lil' squirt runnin' around the place," he says, smiling with his stained teeth hidden behind his beard.

"Yeah. I do remember those days. Have you seen my sister around town? I know she didn't work here much longer after my mom passed." I move to take a sip of the beer.

"No… No. Not really. She stuck around a couple of months, then ran off to your dad's fishing charter down in Florida for the tourists. Got herself married up to some rich local down there and hasn't been back since. What about you? Your mom always bragged on and on how you got yourself a nice chesty blonde in uniform that you were gonna marry before you got out of the Navy."

"Sorry to tell ya, Don, but that ship has sailed. More like sunk and burned up." All I can do is give a fake smile back and try to cover it with another sip of my beer.

"Ahh, horseshit… Don't let some gash get ya down. Plenty of fish in the sea kid," he says as he reaches across the table to slap my shoulder. He just sits back and smiles from ear to ear. "Your mom was proud of you no matter what, Isaac." He leans over to look at the crowd cheering on the game.

"I don't wanna be a burden. I know you're working solo these days."

"Ahh, well. These ol' farts won't wander back to the bar 'til half time anyways. So, what's the plan now? You got a place to stay, or what?" he asks, while lighting up a cigarette.

"Well, not at the moment. I saved up plenty while I was away. But it might be enough to buy an elaborate cardboard box, at the most 'round here."

He flicks his ash into the tray on the table in front of me. "You're always good to stay in one of the rooms upstairs 'til you get on your feet, Isaac. You know that."

I take another swig of beer, but with a struggle as it goes down the wrong pipe. Once I'm done coughing from that and his second-hand smoke, I look back to see him shaking his head at me. "Navy make ya' a lightweight, kid?"

"No… No…" as I grin at his sarcasm. "No, I was looking to catch one of the commercial charters headed out before the season ends. Do you know of any skippers looking for a spare deckhand?"

"Boy, your momma would turn in her grave if she knew you were thinkin' about headin' out this late in the damn season," he says, while shaking his head in concern.

"I know. I know. It's just this once, though. Probably the last one if the catch is good enough and I can get my own place. Find something steadier on the docks after that, ya know?"

"The only skipper I know looking for a greenhorn sits over there in the corner. Name's Captain Walsh. Got a good strong trawler too, last I heard. You be sure to let me know if you head out with any of them," and he points in the skipper's direction.

"Right… Right…" I tell him as he gets up in a feeble struggle from the bench. "Ok, Don. Good to see you again," and raise my glass to him again before finishing my drink.

I get up and walk to the bar and slide Don a ten for the few drinks we shared while he isn't looking. The corner the captain sits in is filled with more smoke than the rest of the place because of the cigar he puffs away at. He glares at me with hateful eyes at first, but I play it off as just his normal demeanor. Most of these crusty old seamen aren't pleasant to be around 'til they've had a few drinks in them.

"Hello sir. Captain Walsh, I was told by Donovan, the owner. My name is Isaac. Could I buy you a drink for a moment of your time?"

He looks me up and down and sets his cigar aside before shaking my hand. He motions me to sit down on the other side of the table. "Get me another lager and earn yourself an interview, kid. Don already told me you might come over here."

He finishes the last of his current drink and wipes it off his dark, bushy mustache. I catch a glimpse of jailhouse tattoos on his knuckles and the top of one hand before he goes for his cigar again. Then, I get a better visual of him with the low lights of the bar. Possibly late forties, but a hard life and too many seasons of rough seas have aged him to have the look of late fifties, more or less. I wave to Don and point out what the captain is drinking so he can bring him another on me. I settle in my seat and he just keeps a tense look towards me. Not a single flinch or movement from him under that worn down New England Patriots hat with a bent fishhook to hold the torn fabric in place at the end of the bill.

"So, tell me your experience with commercial fishing. We need a greenhorn, but I ain't desperate enough this late in the season to hold anybody's hand, either."

"Well… My dad ran a fishing charter for the tourists, and I was with him a lot for the summers when…"

"We ain't out there whale watchin' for the yuppies," he says, interrupting me sternly. Don brings him another lager, and the captain goes right into his drink without hesitation. Don continues to hover over us for a moment to listen in.

I try to justify my efforts with this captain, but I get the feeling he wants no part of it already. "I know sir. But I can cut and clean anything you haul in if that's what you do. I'm a fast learner, too."

Don chimes in before walking away, "He was in the Navy too, Walsh. This here is Andrea's boy. He just got back."

The captain just looks up at him and gives a nod before he walks away. "I remember you. Mainly your mom when she worked here anyway. What did you do in the Navy, kid?"

"I was on an aircraft carrier working towards being IDC but stayed on as a hospital corpsman after basic."

He just raises his hand with the cigar to signal me to shut up while shaking his head before another drink. "Speak fuckin' English, kid. I don't care to know what any of that shit means."

"Medic… I was like a medic in the Navy."

"Ok… Now we're getting somewhere. We lost the last guy we had that knew how to do more than just slap a band-aid on a broken leg. Have you ever been on a real commercial fishing charter before?"

I shake my head yes. "Oh yeah… I did it for the entire summer after high school before I shipped out for the Navy. It was a smaller boat that had the gillnetting set up. It was over six years ago, but I'd like to think I'd just need a refresher instead of a crash course."

He responds with a slight chuckle under his breath, but it really doesn't change his overall bearing. "Well, that's a step up beyond some of the other candidates I've seen the last few days. My freezer ship is outfitted to do dragging to max out our haul every season. We run a tight crew and most of them have been with me for a few years now. You got a wife or kids or anything like that?"

"No sir. It's just me and my one duffle bag with everything I own at the moment."

He leans in, looking closer at me and shifts his head to the side in slight confusion. "You runnin' from the law or somethin', kid? AWOL or some shit like that?"

Stunned by his question, "No... No, I'm not running from anything. I'd actually like to think I'm looking for something... I guess."

"That makes zero sense," he says.

"It makes perfect sense to me, sir."

"Really?" he asks, raising his brow for the first time throughout the conversation.

"Yes, sir. I think maybe I just gotta get lost before I can find it."

He takes a few puffs of his cigar and just stares at me quietly before he speaks up again. "She calls for you, doesn't she?"

Such an elusive question that I don't know how to answer right away. "I'm... I'm not sure who or what you mean," while giving him a puzzled look.

"Sure, you do, kid," as he points his hand with the cigar at me. "Sure, you do... I've seen that look before. Bet I had it too at some point younger than you. Especially when she calls for you."

He just looks at me through the cigar smoke looming around both of us now. In some strange manner, I feel this salty old sea dog is right, but I cannot be for certain.

"I expect my crew to be on the boat the night prior to setting out. They can hobble in drunk as a skunk if they want, but I prefer them to be there and ready for the following day to sober up as we steam out to the fishing grounds. That way, they don't get locked up in the drunk tanks before then. We push out for a max of thirty days and we're cut down to about two weeks before the end of the season this time around. If you're not there in the morning with the rest of the guys, then we'll make do without you. It wouldn't be the first time I left someone behind or went out shorthanded. That's all there is to it, kid."

He finishes the rest of his lager in one swooping gulp and gets out of his seat to reach for his wallet.

"Do I need to get any gear or anything?" I ask.

He throws down a twenty on the table to pay for his drinks. "Nope, the last greenhorn was about your size, so you can just use his." He leans in to put out his cigar in the ash tray on the table. "Dock 19. It's the largest trawler there and you can't miss it. You'll catch an Indian lookin' fella already on the boat. Just let him know Captain Walsh sent you as the new greenhorn. We head out tomorrow at dawn."

He leans back in to shake my hand. "I appreciate your service in the Navy, kid. But you gotta understand, this job isn't for everybody. So, you'll have to excuse me for skipping out on the polite gestures. Don't make any sense to get to know somebody unless they see fit to stick around."

Still holding and shaking with an intense grip in his heavily calloused hand, "Thank you, sir. No, I understand. But I really appreciate the opportunity for this, though."

He lets go of my hand, "Right… Heard that same shit before too."

It quickly registers for me as he starts to walk away that I just got hired on a commercial fishing charter as my first job as a Navy veteran. Still shocked, I grab his attention before he is out of earshot. "Sir… Er, Captain Walsh… What was the name of your ship? Just to be sure…"

He turns and shows a slight grin under that mustache for the first time since I met him. As if it is difficult for him to smile, but he can't hold it back when answering. For it may be the only thing he prides himself with.

Especially in hearing how he says,
"She's called The Sea Hellion…"

Chapter 2 - Comanche

Even though my mother's old friend and employer was as nice as can be, I chose not to say goodbye to Don. I didn't want to, in all honesty. It almost makes me feel regrettable to have come here and make my presence known, just to become yet another fading memory of better days for all of us. In a selfish sense, my memories there of me and my friends during our childhood years are still innocent to this day, and I prefer to always keep them as such. I can hear the bar patrons cheering or cursing at the game on the TVs as I make my way outside unnoticed. A slight breeze of colder air from the ocean drops the temps at night. All seems quiet during my lone walk down empty streets. I only hear the sea whispering with light splashes against the small fishing piers for the locals.

The docks are a poorly lit area. All the boats appear to have a heavy dinge and grunginess to them under the haze of the lamps that put out more of a yellow fog than an actual level of visibility. My former fiancé's smile exits my mind when I reach the docking point for The Sea Hellion. And she is a massive trawler, extending almost a hundred feet or so. I can see the resemblance of an older Chinese trawler from the overall appearance, but it's nothing like the smaller tourist fishing charters my dad would take out. She's older and more decrepit than the others. The main wheelhouse area sits closer to the stern with the huge pulley arms for the trawl nets at the end. The dark gray painted exterior has rust and decay in multiple areas, especially where the anchor is released. A few lights are on at the front of the deck, and I see the captain looking down at something in the wheelhouse. So, I make my way up the temporary scaffolding system with my duffle strapped to my back. The deck of the ship is cluttered with cables, anchor chains, and loose netting.

I look up to wave down the captain, just when I am thrusted down to the deck without warning.

"What the…!!!" I yell, as I try to get back on my feet.

A massive brute of a man is coming right at me before I can get the captain's attention. He grunts viciously as he lifts me up by my duffle, still strapped to my back.

"Shit!... Shit!..."

He's dragging me over to the other side of the ship. Dragging me at first until my feet are lifted off the deck and I'm flailing around trying to kick him. He bashes straight through cables and barrels placed on the deck. I kick one of them in my struggle, hoping to get the captain's attention above. He heads straight for the railing and turns me around as my duffle and backside are now leaning over the side. His powerful hands grip the collar of my jacket. Tribal style tattoos cover his face as he leans in closer to me, just to bare his teeth and growl with a crazed stare.

He holds me up with one hand and throws my legs over the railing. I'm about to be thrown over. "Wait!?!?... Wait!?!?... Wait!!!"

His arms are outstretched, and I try to reach for his jacket, but resort to holding on to his forearms in case he lets his grip off my jacket.

"*COMANCHE!*" a familiar voice yells across the loudspeaker. We both look over at the wheelhouse and my feet are still dangling around in the air like struggling fish out of water. *"Put him down, Comanche. He's the new guy."* The speakers whir after the captain moves the mic away from his mouth.

He lifts me back up over the rails with ease and just looks down at me as my feet slowly touch the hardwood deck. As soon as he lets go, I straighten my jacket up and drop my duffle down. In a fit of anger, I lunge at him to shove him away from me. But it's no use. He must be pushing three-hundred pounds of pure brawn. His hands are cupped into a fist, but I send my solid left jab at his already flattened nose. He doesn't so much as flinch at that first direct hit to his face. I keep my arms and fists up, ready for a hard hit to come right back at me. But he goes to lift me off my feet again.

The captain's voice comes over the loudspeaker again, *"Dammit Comanche! Stop messing with the new guy and clean that mess up!"*

He throws me down on the deck like a rag doll. At least I land closer to the steps that lead up to the wheelhouse. He tosses my duffle in my direction before he turns away to put the barrels we knocked over back in place.

"Get up here, stupid. Before I let him throw a punch back at ya that you won't wake up from," says the captain. I can hear him chuckling under his breath before he moves the mic for the loudspeaker away from his mouth. I look back and forth at this giant and the wheelhouse as I make my way towards the steps. He stands perfectly still just to glare at me for what seems an eternity, before committing to lift the cluster of barrels back into place. I keep an eye on him all the way up the steps to the wheelhouse.

"I see you and Comanche are off to a good start," says the captain, as I open the door to let myself in quickly. We both look down at the deck to see him muscle around the barrels and cables as if they're weightless. "Don't let him fool you, kid. He may look like a big Indian ox, but he knows more English than he lets on. He just chooses not to talk much."

"Is he really Native American? Like a full-on Comanche tribesman or...?"

"Gotta stop you there..." He reaches under the dashboard for various paperwork. He keeps looking over it while still talking to me. "We don't know. He's been with us for a while now. In fact, he's been with me the second longest, even before I leased this new ship from the charter. And yes, he would have thrown you overboard if I hadn't of said anything."

"Sounds like a nice guy then, sir."

"He's nicer than most," he says, as he hands over a stack of paperwork. "Fill this out. It's the application we keep on file for the main office of the charter but consider yourself hired on as long as you're still here in the morning when we head out. It's gonna be a few days to push out to the Grand Banks, maybe sooner weather depending, but a lot of things need to happen before we get to the fishing grounds. Two meals a day and get as much rest as you can before then. Once the first net comes up, it can be upwards of a twenty-hour day for about a week or until we meet our quota for the rest of the season. Plenty of time for questions and answers from the crew on the way out there and you best know what you're expected to do when we get there. Don't come to me directly for anything from this point forward. If you got a problem, you talk to the deck boss, then he talks to me. Understood?"

He sits down in the captain's chair and props his feet up on an empty space near the dash controls. An unfinished smelly cigar is lit back up as he looks away from me out into the darkness of the bay through the back windows of the wheelhouse.

"You'll get greenhorn share from the haul for the first and second outings, then bump up to deckhand share for the third. That's the way it works for all first timers. You slack off while we're out there, your share gets cut in half and I split it up between the rest of us who picked up your slack. You do good work out there and you can earn yourself a spot with the crew. A lot of our fishing grounds are dried up. So, sometimes we're a bust and we just stay out there 'til I find the fish. It's that simple, kid. Get that paperwork to me first thing in the mornin', if you're still here, and I'll fax it back to the main office as we head out. The most important thing is your emergency contacts. Comanche will show you around the ship and to your bunk. Try not to piss him off again."

"Yes, sir... Wait... Where did he go?" I ask, while looking down at the deck. He just points at the door with his back still facing me. I turn around to see Comanche hovering over us at the doorway and I shudder in my boots. "Whoa? How long have you been standing there?" I look back over at the captain with his back still facing us. Small puffs of smoke start to fill the air and he says nothing more. I turn back to Comanche and gather enough spine to reach my hand out a try to shake his.

"Hello. I'm Isaac." He just stares down at me again. With a slight growl towards me while shaking his head, he bends down to grab my duffle, ignoring my attempt at a handshake. He goes to walk out of the wheelhouse with my duffle. I guess I'm supposed to follow him. I turn to the captain in an attempt at some comic relief. "He sure is a pleasant guy. Ain't he, Captain?"

"It's Skipper, or Skipper Walsh. I'll let the rest of the crew know there's a newbie in the empty bunk and they won't bug you. Now get the fuck outta my wheelhouse and stay below deck for a while."

I turn to follow Comanche down the steps of the wheelhouse. He leads me through a maze of corridors below deck to get to the cramped-up room with several bunks stacked up like sardines. The smell that comes from the single stall bathroom next to it almost burns my nose hairs. Before he leads me in, I catch another festering aroma of fish decay further down below deck.

My attention turns back to Comanche as he keeps staring me up and down, just less aggressively this time. He raises a single massive arm upright with my duffle appearing weightless in his hand. It gets deliberately dropped on an empty mattress.

"You... Bunk here," he says, as he walks by me out of the bunk room.

I shake my head yes in understanding, but he doesn't even turn his back to look at me again while walking away. The dim light only allows so much view in here. Each bunk, stacked about four high, has a small drawer unit underneath. Several pockets are on the interior of the bunk area, and it seems familiar to me compared to my weeks at sea on the aircraft carriers. The major difference is the ash trays left in several cup holders outside each bunk, along with the graffitied cursing and naked women taped to the walls of the bunks that have an occupier. Ashes and cigarette burns are all over the floor under my feet. My new bunk, second from the top, was left empty but tidy, with a small pillow and fresh linen tucked in.

Then I realize that I forgot to ask why the last greenhorn didn't stick around. I step out into the hallway and grab Comanche's attention before he leaves to wherever he's going.

"Hey... Comanche..."

He turns around before heading back up the steps that lead to the deck, but all I get from him is a grunt, acknowledging that I have his attention again.

"What happened to the last greenhorn you guys had? He just didn't work out, or…?"

He menacingly walks back towards me as I stand in the doorway of the bunk room. My heart skips a beat when he reaches behind him and pulls out a massive bowie knife in a manner that would make most people shit themselves. I move a foot closer to the door in case I have to slam it shut in his face, but I hold my ground.

He stops in front of me and raises his empty hand closer to my face and looks at me, knowing how tense and confused I am.

"Hand," he says.

He swings his knife in front of his empty hand but lowers it before it catches the blade. When that blade moves by my face, I can hear it cutting through the air.

"Hand… Gone," he says.

"You're saying his hand was cut really bad? Like in an accident while out at sea? Cut by lines or ropes, or something like that, right? Is that what you're telling me?"

He just smiles and picks at his bare teeth with that massive knife.

He shakes his head no, "No… Gone," and he motions his hands to disappear again.

"Gone as in chopped off?" I ask him, still trying to hold my ground in the doorway with this giant in my face waving a huge bowie knife around.

He glares and leans in closer. "Gone…"

Chapter 3 - Stowaways

What little I carry manages to fit into the single drawer under the bunk easily. My instrument case sits snugly at the foot end of the bunk without issue. Once I jump in and stretch my legs, I speed through most of the paperwork. It's all the standard information on a typical application. Then I hit a blank spot to fill in information I don't have. The most critical piece of information, according to the skipper, and I don't know what to write down. Direct deposit stuff, driver license info for background checks that never happen, prior employers for referral calls that also never happen, but I draw a blank when I can't think of anyone for an emergency contact. There's simply nothing to write.

Everybody I knew in the Navy doesn't even know I'm here or where I went. It bothers me at first as I zone out looking at the various blank spots on the forms. Then, a sense of relief comes over me and I accept the fact that I really have gotten away from it all. The skipper may not like it, but I don't think they expect him to look into any of it on his part. The only contact info I write is Donavan's address and phone number for the ol' pub. Hopefully he knows to bury me next to my mom if anything happens while I'm out here.

It's getting late, so I switch off the tiny dome light above me and hop out of the bunk. Some fresh air and a smoke would be good before calling it a night. I would like to be asleep versus acting like I'm asleep when the rest of the crew comes in for the night to avoid any awkwardness. This room could only start smelling worse when they all come back in. Outside the room, I take a look at the coat racks for all the rain gear. Hats, gloves, pants, jackets, and wet shoes all lined up smelling of fish guts and saltwater. Most of them are the color orange. One of them clearly belongs to Comanche based on its size, but there is one green one and one red one. I do remember seeing a blue set in the wheelhouse too. The green one, as it is currently the cleanest one, is usually for the most inexperienced member of the crew so they can keep a closer eye on the newbie. That's only an assumption from the last time I went out on a commercial fishing charter before the Navy.

The fresh air fills my nostrils in a hurry. The deck is quiet and still lowly lit. Even the wheelhouse has the lights off. I walk around the deck to take a dim look at some of the gear. The winch for the dragnet is massive, strong enough to bring in several hundred pounds of fish at a time. Netting is stacked up higher than my head and tied down. Small buoys and barrels are strewn about in various places. I find a spot to sit near the portside edge of the boat that faces the water and cast a shadow of myself when a flick my lighter. I sit and listen to the ripples of the water coming in and splash against the side of the boat. The waves hit the shoreline nearby and I look up to see an open section of stars surrounded by overcast. Not much moonlight to see the ship better, just the yellow dim light from the docks behind me.

The cherry of my cigarette drops off halfway through my smoke. I quickly step it out with my shoe. I flick my lighter several times to relight. Now my lighter is shittin' out on me. Each flick of the lighter reveals a dark spot at the bow of the ship. A dark spot not colored in the same manner as the rest of the netting and fishing gear. More like a light fabric fluttering in the wind, even though there is only a slight breeze. A black fabric moving unnaturally somehow, and I can't make it out. My lighter won't stay lit long enough to see what it is. Other than the gray steel of the ship, nothing else had that dark of a color when I came on board and the lights of the wheelhouse were still on, or maybe I just didn't see it then because I was almost thrown over by Comanche. The dark fabric moves suddenly, like that of a person sidestepping closer to the edge.

"Hello?"

The shadowy figure stops moving. Too small to be Comanche and not the stance of the skipper, either. That's a woman's dress that flutters around in the darkness. Maybe her hair, too.

"Miss? Are you one of the crew?"

I give up on my lighter and slowly step toward her. She's not dressed like any sailor. She just keeps her back to me, but the sounds of the tides, coming in and out, grow louder the closer I get to her. Her head turns slightly, and I see pale white skin on the side of her face partially covered by long dark hair. My eyes may be tricking me from my lack of sleep while traveling from one bus station to the next, but my ears don't fool me. I can hear her trying to talk to me with her back turned, but it sounds more like a whisper. The waves and current hits the beachside harder.

"Miss...?" I ask her, in hopes that she'll turn around towards me so I can hear her better.

A thud comes from across the other side of the boat, closer to the docks. A man with a yellow rain jacket points a flashlight at me with a half-smoked cigarette still in my mouth. He walks closer with deliberate steps.

"A Mister Skipper Walsh... Yes?" he asks harshly with a Spanish accent and broken English. I can't get a good glimpse at him with his light shining in my face, but I shake my head no and point to the wheelhouse. He looks up and the skipper's wheelhouse lights are back on, so he walks back in that direction. Head to toe in yellow rain gear and his fresh rubber boots squeak across the deck on his way to the stairs.

I turn back to look for the whispering lady I was talking to, but she's gone. I step closer to see loose black tarping draped over the railing and perfectly still. Tarp wouldn't move like that with the breeze. I know I didn't sleep much on the bus. I've seen some strange things out at sea on the Naval ships having no sleep for two or three days at a time. But nothing like that of a draped tarp playing tricks on me in the shadows on deck. I'll know in the morning if there is a lady on the crew somewhere.

The Hispanic and the skipper talk a while in the wheelhouse, and Comanche comes up from below deck to see them talking too. I don't care how dark it may be. You could see a man the size of Comanche a mile away. How the hell does he fit in one of those bunks? The skipper makes his way out of the wheelhouse with the man in yellow. Comanche just waves me over as we both watch what the skipper is doing with the stranger that even Comanche appears bothered to see. I take one last look at the draped tarping before walking over to the door to head below deck with Comanche.

"Is he one of the crew members? And I just saw a lady out on deck somewhere... Or I think I did?" I ask Comanche.

He just grunts and shakes his head no. "Yellow Jack." He says nothing else but seems more disgusted than just disgruntled at the person in the wheelhouse with the skipper.

Comanche and I make our way down a few steps to head below, but I look back to see the skipper and this *Yellow Jack*, as Comanche calls him, start moving several large duffel bags from the scaffolding and onto the boat. Two in each hand for the both of them. Neither of them notices me or Comanche already making our way down the stairs. I toss my half-smoked cigarette over the side and follow him back to the bunk room.

"Comanche...? Wait... Is that your real name?" He just looks up at me as he takes his boots off in the hallway. "Well... Who was that guy? You've seen him before, right? What were him and the skipper carrying onboard? Is he a regular with the crew or...?"

He just shakes his head at me, but I can't tell if he is answering no to one or all of my questions.

All he says, while pointing at the bunks, is, "You sleep..."

Well, that answers a whole lot of nothing. I slip my boots off and watch Comanche somehow squeeze himself into the bunk on the other side of me. I can tell he struggles a bit but seems used to not being able to stretch his legs all the way out. The bunk shifts and squeaks as he adjusts his massive frame with no headroom. He turns the lights out and closes his privacy curtain.

"Well, I bid you a goodnight then, Comanche..." I tell him sarcastically.

Nothing back from him. I'd like to think the rest of the crew is more approachable. I know these guys can be rough on newbies the first time out with them, but that's the norm of things. In an effort to get some sleep, I climb into my bunk and close the curtains too. Even with my stomach reminding me of the lack of a decent meal in days, closing my eyes comes easily. Especially with the thought of more freedoms and no ridiculous rollcalls first thing in the mornings. No more entitled and demanding officers walking around that don't know how to lead a group of sailors out of a wet paper bag. This is all familiar, just a lot better, sort of. I remember my first time out on a fishing charter was hard work for days at a time, but we would see the fruits of our labors. Our efforts on these ships aren't in place just to make the Naval officers look better for someone more important than them. Am I being too optimistic to think I could definitely get used to this? Why question a good thing?

The door that leads to the deck is slammed open, followed by the sound of men shuffling their feet and low laughter. I slightly open my curtain to look around and see the commotion. A group of three men, all reeking of liquor and cheap cigarettes, come trotting down the stairs like a herd of elephants. They all laugh low at first but can't seem to contain themselves in their drunken stupor.

"Dammit Scotty. You could have had that ol' cougar. I'm tellin' ya, you could have had her. She was all over you. Chicks dig the whole accent thing. You could've let her bring you back to being straight again," one says loudly.

"It's not my fancy to be bedding down with the Crypt Keeper. Aye," he answers in a Scottish accent. They all laugh and chuckle more in the hallway.

"Keep it down you two. Diesel's gonna try to bring that hairy behemoth girl he loves onboard and pork her senseless again. I need to at least watch for some motivation to drain the lizard with before I head out to sea with you degenerates."

Oh Christ. Now I know why Comanche just wanted me to go to bed and close the curtains. I wish I was sound asleep, not to hear what I think is coming. Not this type of crap all over again. I thought those days were finally over.

"*Not my fancy*, says the gay Scotsman. Well, at least I got a good handsy from the seventeen-year-old barkeep before we left."

"Fuck you, Iceman. Call me gay again, ya damn Yank. Are you sure that wasn't your cousin reachin' under the table just to be lookin' for ya frozen lil' pecker, aye?"

"I'll give you that, Scotsman. But she wasn't as good as your mom the other night, 'cause she definitely found it!"

And they both start laughing at each other obnoxiously, just for the third older guy to put a stop to it as they try to malinger into their bunks. "You two knock it off. Get in bed and close your curtains. I can hear her laughing with him. There coming down now. Just shut it, will ya?!"

They chuckle and scurry like cockroaches to get into their bunks in a hurry. There's only one problem. The only open bunk after they settle in and close their curtains is the bunk directly below mine. This cannot be happening right now. But I hear a female giggling as a man's voice talks low to her down the hallway. They both stumble around before they make it into the bunk room and lean up against my bed and the one above me. The only thing I can think right now is to cover my ears and hope these curtains are strong enough to not fall down if they accidentally grab it in their moment of grotesque passion and moaning.

"Oh, baby Boo, do you have to head out again this time of the year? We got plenty to make it through the winter," says the woman, while I still hear them slobbering all over each other and swapping spit.

"Not if we want that new minivan you liked for you and all the kids. Besides, you got me now and we can rock the boat all to ourselves with the babysitter at home."

Oh, fucking Christ. This is really happening. They moan and suck on each other more than they whisper sweet nothings to each other. All I want is just for this to end quickly, like it normally does when this happens. I try to close my curtain all the way, but one of her ass cheeks is propped up on it. I just roll over and try to cover my ears with my sad excuse for a pillow and act like I'm not here. Luckily, they squirm down to the bunk underneath mine. I have no idea how they both even fit under there, but the occasional kick under my bed tells me they don't both fit under there. More grunts and moans and random hits to the bottom of my bunk become faster and more frequent.

"Fill me up with that diesel, baby Boo! Fill me up like you do!"

"Oooooh yeah, I got ya baby girl!!! You want it all?!?!"

"Oh my God, yes!!!... Yes!!!"

The moaning, the sucking, and sound of bodily fluids getting exchanged can usually be ignored with some ear buds. But when a lady screams at the top of her lungs as her man gets off to *"fill me up with all your diesel, baby Boo"* I digress into knowing the quiet is slowly approaching when they both finally finish. I couldn't be more wrong, though. It goes on for hours into the night on multiple occasions, without even a single break.

On one hand, I want to give the man she calls *Diesel* a handshake with some serious kudos for that consistent level of performance and continued stamina. After all, it's good to know that even the rest of us have a chance when returning to port, especially if this guy can get laid that good. On the other hand, this is an awkwardly familiar experience from being back on the aircraft carriers for the Navy. At least we would try to be a lot quieter about it when sneaking a girl in with you back into the male bunk racks.

Chapter 4 - Shipping Out

That had to have been the worst night of sleep I've had in a long time. I try to avoid stepping on the two obnoxious lovers in the bunk underneath me. He's lays next to her with his legs smothered by her thick thighs, still naked as the day they were born. A slutty tramp stamp distorted from stretch marks is visible on her lower back. I don't think they made any effort to cover themselves last night in their drunken love fest. More power to them both, I guess. At least somebody is getting laid on a regular basis when at port.

I slip my boots on and head up from below deck and see the skies are more clear than yesterday. They may even be blue today, but more important is the fresh air that fills my lungs. Comanche already sits by the side of the steps near the narrow stairway that heads up to the wheelhouse. He sits patiently covered in a blanket to stay warm in the brisk morning breeze as he stares outwards. His ponytail slightly flaps in the wind as he puffs on a long pipe. He only glares at me as I approach him to recover from our first encounter from when he almost threw me overboard.

"Hey there, Comanche. Get a good sleep last night?" I ask, while walking up to him.

He just blankly stares at me and takes in a long smoke from his pipe.

"Right, Right dumb question… Well anyway, listen, I think we got off on the wrong foot last night and… And, well…"

But he just keeps giving me that blank stare. Even when I reach out my hand to shake his, yet again, he ignores it. Now he doesn't even look at me.

"Ya know… I'm the one that should be pissed off here. You tried to throw me overboard, man. I mean, what the hell?"

He just raises his finger at me and shakes his head. A nice way to tell me to shut up, I assume. Then he points toward what he is looking at over the side of the boat on the docks. Skipper Walsh is talking to a woman slightly younger than him. And boy, she does not look happy with him at all as Comanche and I listen in.

"I don't care what you think… I just want you to help take care of your kids like the courts told you," she says to him sternly.

He mumbles something back out of earshot as he looks around to make sure he doesn't have an audience, but he doesn't think to look back at Comanche and me looking over the side of the ship.

She keeps talking to him, but it turns to more like a gripe session directed at the skipper. "You said that last time. You say that every time that this is the last time, but you keep doing it anyway! These people don't care for you and I don't care for our kids to know you either if you stay involved with these people!"

The skipper motions with his hands to get her to lower her voice, but even I know women enough to remember not to tell them that. It's like an invitation for them to get louder and more pissed off.

"Don't tell me what to do, asshole! I'm not your fuckin' wife anymore and I don't have to listen to you! You have to listen to me and if you don't, the courts will make you listen then," she yells, pointing her finger at him like a troubled child.

The skipper goes to pull an envelope out of his back pocket and hand it to her. Without warning, she slaps the envelope out of his hand and goes to shove him away. She shoves him again and he just takes it. She even slaps him in the face, knocking his hat off onto the dock too. Comanche and I just look at each other and cringe under our breath after seeing an epic slap like that.

"I don't want your filthy money! Get out there and go catch some fish and make some honest money for your kids, you fuckin' loser. You're lucky I don't tell the courts what you're into out there. Then my kids will never see their worthless Daddy again!" She turns to stomp away on the docks yelling, "Loser! You're a fuckin' loser!!"

The skipper just stands there for a second to watch her walk away. Then he bends over to collect his hat and the envelope he tried to give her.

Comanche taps my shoulder, and we walk over to the other side of the boat to act like we just came up from below deck before the skipper gets back up on the boat. We both prop up against some of the netting gear and barrels.

"Was that like his ex-wife or somethin'?" I ask, Comanche.

He shakes his head yes as he smokes his pipe and put two fingers up.

"Two ex-wives. The skipper has two ex-wives or baby mommas? Is the other one that pissed off with him too?"

Comanche just shakes his head and shrugs his shoulders with a straight face. The only thing he says between a drag of his smoke pipe is, "Women…"

Not much to say to that on either of our parts. It's more like a mutual understanding. There's really nothing else to add to it.

The skipper finally comes up from the docks and sees both of us on the other side of the boat. "You're still here?" he asks me. I just shake my head yes, then he turns to look at Comanche. "Are the rest of the guys awake yet? We're shipping out soon."

Comanche just shakes his head no at him and Skipper Walsh just glares back at us as he walks closer to the door to head below. I stand up real fast to say something, hoping to spare him the headache of discovering a bimbo stashed away on his boat. Comanche just taps my shoulder again to have me restrain myself from opening my mouth as the skipper walks down below. "Get the lines brought in, Comanche. We leave as soon as these bozos get up and dressed..." he says, before we're out of earshot. I look over at Comanche and he holds a finger to his lips and shakes his head again, but he has a slight grin this time. This is about to get ugly for all the guys still sleeping in the bunks. I will admit, I am glad I'm not still down there trying to sleep in when the captain...

"GOD DAMMIT!!! What the hell are you doing in here again?!?!" yells the skipper from below. I look around to see other sailors in neighboring boats docked next to us come up from below or out of their wheelhouses to see what the yelling is about. "Diesel!!! You lil' shit… Get this fuckin' land whale off my boat now. RIGHT FUCKIN' NOW!!!"

Grunting and stomping below deck begins as Comanche and I sit and watch the train wreck about unfold. The woman yells out back at the skipper and then back at her man. "What the fuck Diesel! You said the boat was empty for the night! Hey… Where are you going with my damn clothes, asshole?"

"We're headed out today, Boo."

"You lil' lying sack of shit!... How long have these guys been in here? Were they here last night too?!?!"

The other guys laugh and one of them, an older one with an unlit half a cigarette hanging out of his mouth, stumbles up from below deck while still trying to put his boots on. The captain follows closely behind with the set of clothes and a single sneaker in hand. He walks over to the docking side of the boat and throws them over onto the docks. My first thought is that he is throwing over the belongings of the man that brought a hooker on board just to screw her senseless last night. But when I see a massive bra get thrown over with the rest of the clothes, my stomach turns in knowing she is about to walk up from below in the nude and in a fury at the captain, or her boyfriend, or maybe even both?

I hear more commotion as they make their way up to the deck, and it sounds like someone is getting slapped in the back of the head.

"Ow… Ahh! Shit, Boo… Why you gotta always be so bitchy in the morning?"

And the one they call Diesel comes up with his large white lady behind him, smacking his back and neck with the other sneaker. His pants are still undone, and his shirt is missing. He tries to block each of her minor swats, but she makes a few solid hits on his skull. She isn't too concerned with covering up her naked body with a random raincoat that she must have grabbed from the hallway. Two other guys come up behind them, laughing like frat boys, and dash out of her way as she continues to hit Diesel in the back of his head. Her thunder thighs show no signs of being able to fit under that coat. A massive, and saggy double D tit falls out to aid in her assault against her late-night lover while she flails around looking for a good shot at him with her shoe. One solid hit with one of those knockers can send a guy to the hospital in a coma. I guess there are worse ways to get your lights knocked out.

"You lyin' sack of fuckin' shit!" She keeps swinging at him as they both rush off the boat and the others look on and laugh. Her belly jiggles all over the place as she throws one of her huge legs over the side to keep chasing after him. As soon as that big old thigh is lifted over the side, we all catch a cringeworthy sighting of her bush. "Yeah! Yeah!... Take a good look at it, you damn perverts!" She yells at all of us.

"God dammit, Diesel! You bring her on the boat like that again, and I'll drop your skinny black ass off in the middle of the Atlantic." Skipper Walsh turns to the rest of us. Comanche and I are somewhat still, but the other crewmembers are still laughing like schoolboys. "I thought I told you guys to bring in the lines. Get it done now. Fuckin' shows over. Make it happen, Dick!" he says to one of the guys that came up from below in all the commotion.

Most of us rush over to the side of the boat to bring in the lines. I look at Comanche as he muscles in some of the thick ropes. "Diesel's girlfriend seems nice, yeah?" I ask him in sarcasm.

He just grunts while struggling to pull in the ropes and shakes his head no. "Women…" he says.

I take a second, but I think I understand what he's getting at now. "Right… Women… I get it."

I look up above him and see the skipper going inside the wheelhouse to start up the engines. Right next to him is the Hispanic one that Comanche calls Yellow Jack, who must have also watched the morning's entertainment.

"Unhook that scaffolding," yells the one the skipper called Dick. "And Diesel, get your ass up here if you're coming. We got some fuckin' fish to catch, lover boy."

I hop over the side to unhook the scaffolding stairs we used to get on and off the boat when docked. Diesel and his lady are fully dressed now, but she still fusses at him. I look on as I unravel more ropes and hooks from the side of the ship, wondering if he's about to get slapped in the face like the skipper did earlier. Instead, he helps her finish getting dressed in a sweater pulling it over her chest. She still yells at him in the process until he leans in and gives her a sloppy kiss. She holds him tight. It's like a passionate teenage fling in high school, full of all the drama and excitement. They hate each other when things go wrong and love each other deeply when nobody is looking. It's kinda sweet actually, in a very weird way. He lets her go, and she resumes to cursing at him again.

The engines rumble on as we bring in the last of the ropes holding us to the dock. Diesel runs up the scaffolding as we start to push away, and his lady becomes even more furious.

"You lying fuckin' prick! Get your skinny black ass back down here now!!!"

He jumps on board and another crewman hands him his dingy shirt. He leans over the side to yell back at her while we push further and further away from the docks. He waves his shirt around in circles at her,

"Farwell my love!! Upon my return I shall fill you again with all the lil' Diesels in the world!" He keeps laughing at her dismay.

"You sack of shit!!!" She takes her single shoe back off to throw it at the boat, thudding against the hull and splashing down to the water below.

"I love you too, my baby Boo!" he says.

"I'll be waiting right here when you get back shit head!!!" She yells louder as we glide further away.

"I know!!" He laughs as he puts his shirt back on.

She finally stomps away, now barefoot, still cursing him and flipping off some of the nosey onlookers from the neighboring boats parked in the docks beside us.

Diesel turns around to catch his first look at me. He is a thin and frail looking black man at first glance but seems as if he would be a bit too squirrelly to catch. Then he smiles as he pulls out a pack of Kools from his pants pocket. His smile is filled with brown teeth, but it's more like a cluster of gold and silver teeth holding his cigarette in place as he walks over to greet me. Not a single pound of meat on his bones, and I wonder how he is keeping warm with the chilly breeze.

"Hey there Dick, we got us another greenhorn, yeah?" he asks the other crewman near the crane levers.

"I guess so Diesel. The skipper picked him up at the pub last night."

All the other guys seem busy enough, so I drop the anchor ropes I was rolling away and attempt to make a better first impression than I did with Comanche. "Name's Isaac, sir," as I reach out my hand to shake his.

He shakes my hand hard, with a surprising grip for such a smaller person. "Name's Diesel there Greenhorn. You best wash that hand. You already know where it's been last night."

He laughs as I jerk my hand out of his in disgust. "Awe man, what the hell?" I say, as I go back to stowing in the last of the ropes.

"Now, wait... wait there now, Greenhorn. Best get a good whiff of that before you wash it off your mitts, aye?" says the man with a Scottish accent on the other side of the boat. He walks over into sight, moving some smaller buoys around closer to the netting. "Be the best whiff of something pleasant that you get before we all smell like rottin' fish cunt before the trip's end, aye?"

"No thanks…"

We all stay busy while the boat is maneuvered out of the port area. I mainly follow Comanche's lead, but I only bother him in aimlessly wandering around trying to help. I vaguely remember this time period of a commercial fishing trip. We set out to sea with petty things to accomplish before reaching the fishing grounds. When we're done fishing the goal is to have everything cleaned up and back in place before we return to port. That way, the boat is ready to depart again as quickly as possible once we offload the catch. Of course, most crewmen take some variation of a shore leave for a couple of days before heading back out again to handle their personnel affairs and restock on supplies. And obviously, see their families, have a few drinks, and blow off a load in the significant other like we already know who.

It's chill time with few duties to handle right now on our way out. Get a few decent meals a day and more sleep than most would get in a typical nine-to-five workweek. But once the net goes down for the drag, it's non-stop for days at a time. Up to two or three days without stopping. The docks and the port area disappears behind the fog first. Then the waves of seagulls come out to look for a free meal anywhere they can. Smaller tourist charters and whale watchers don't even come out this time of year. The further away from land we get, the more at home I feel. The cold breeze and the smell of salty air brings back many thoughts and memories of a different time. In all reality, they may have been better times. I don't know if I'll make new memories with this crew, but it's worth a shot. They don't seem like a bad bunch. Unapproachable right now while we all take care of minor tasks, but that's the way of it for newbies like me.

It doesn't take long for the cold to really set in. The views of rock clusters with lighthouses mounted on top come and go while the seagulls lose interest in us. I look out back where we just steamed from, and land is out of sight now. A new chapter is beginning, and I hope whatever led me out here isn't just an effort to tarnish and burn the previous chapter. No longer anything to lose, but everything to gain. I might not find a clean slate out here, but just to find something more is what I really came to do and I'm sure I'll find it. These same thoughts run through my mind endlessly these days, it seems. The sea does that to most of us. We forget the sight of life back on land and become lost in her trance. All the while, this rugged and lowly trawler gently steams ahead into gray waters.

Chapter 5 - Initiation

I mention nothing further about the lady in black I saw on the deck the first night on the boat. The thoughts of her were left in my mind as mystic and borderline creepy. The skipper's wife nor Diesel's land whale had the same silhouette as her. To avoid looking like an idiot, I choose to say nothing about her. I didn't even see her face. These old seamen, they have enough stories to tell, I'm sure. It's not necessarily her eerie presence that sticks with me for some reason. It's trying to understand what she was saying before I lost sight of her. I try to direct in my mind to figure out what she whispered that I couldn't fully hear. I played it off the first few nights out here on my lack of sleep before boarding and overthinking things. But her image and whispering voice just won't go away.

The first several days are a blur. Scotty helps me insure my duties as a greenhorn are done to the skipper's liking. With as much as he knows about being a seaman and fishing, he would fit well at the wheelhouse on a ship of his own. Especially, with that older style captains hat he wears with more than enough sea salt grudge at the brim. His accent cracks me up often, but I try to remain serious when he teaches me things. Stowing ropes, washing the decks, fixing the holes throughout the trawl netting, and prepping the buoys. No matter where we go on the ship, kitchen or sleeping quarters, he seems to have a cigarette in his mouth that always ashes down his long unkempt white beard. Apparently, the captain left him to babysit me while we steam out to the fishing grounds. He does seem more approachable than the rest of them. Older and more experienced, too.

The sea tosses us around lightly as we steam further and further out. Still gray but calm for the most part. A breach of blue sky passes through the overcast occasionally and the sunshine warms the deck under my feet. Comanche comes up behind me while working on the nets and points at a knot that I missed. He gives the rest of them a good tug and shakes his head yes.

"Good ties," he says, as he walks away with his imposing footsteps on the deck.

Like the light sway of the ship doesn't even faze him as he walks back down below. I guess it's a good thing to have the most imposing guy on the boat and the most experienced guy on the boat in good graces with you as the newbie. Most of the men are down below. Playing cards and talking their typical sea talk for when they return to port with their share of the catch. I look up at the wheelhouse to see Scotty and the captain talking. Yellow Jack stays up there a lot too with the captain. I only see him come down when he cooks for chow time, but I'm the one that gets to clean up after all of them. And heaven forbid if I don't keep the coffee pots full and brewing all the time, but something has to sober these guys up before we drop down the first net. The one they call Dick always yells at me over that. In fact, he has yet to say anything to me other than yelling to *"keep that coffee brewing fresh, Greenhorn."*

Scotty comes out of the wheelhouse and makes his way down while the captain stays near the wheelhouse entrance above to have a vantage point of the entire deck. I turn to look and see Comanche coming up with the rest of the crew. They suddenly have a serious look on their face, which is a change from the typical smokin' and jokin' they do when work is being done. They all surround behind me as I'm still working on the netting.

"Are we close, aye, Skip?" yells Scotty towards the captain still looking down at us. The skipper just shakes his head yes and points towards the starboard side. He motions for Yellow Jack still in the wheelhouse to bring down the speed of the boat and the engine RPMs lower to a snail's pace on the water.

"Best you have a proper meet and greet of the crew there, greenhorn," says Scotty. "But first, time to earn your shellback."

"Shellback?" I ask, as my shoulders and fists grow tense. God only knows what these guys are up to. But a shellback in the Navy meant some sort of stupid ritual when crossing over the equator for the first time.

"Initiation, Greenhorn. We're crossing into the North Atlantic," says Diesel.

They all surround me, stern and quiet. I have no issue with a bit of hazing. I've given my fair share to others. It's all usually in good fun and spirits, but none of these guys are smiling. I look up at the captain and see he is just as serious as the rest of them. This can't be good. Scotty turns to look up at the skipper and he motions Yellow Jack to stop the boat now.

The sun comes out, pushing through the overcast during the midday hours. Seeing the ocean somewhat blue for the first time in several days should be a good feeling, but with all these guys closing in on me, my appreciation for the hazy blue waters is diminished. They lead me over to the side of the boat and Scotty has a small cup attached to a mop stick in his hand. A few of them look over the side as he reaches down to the water with his makeshift cup and pole.

"There it is," says Diesel with excitement.

I look at all of them as they grow a bit more eager and less tense. I glance over the side of the ship to see what Scotty is reaching for and a small cluster of bubbles is coming to the ocean's surface, surrounding a tiny whirlpool in the water. The ship is moving too slow, and the engines aren't revving enough to be creating bubbles and foam like that. The waters have grown less choppy since the sun came out to blue the water, but wherever those bubbles and the whirlpool is coming from is too dark to see in the blue depths below the ship. He reaches the cup right into the tiny whirlpool.

"Ha, ha, yes… Got it mates!" Scotty yells out in his accent.

He brings the cup in carefully not to spill any of it on the deck. I look at the others as they nudge shoulders with each other, preparing for what's to come. The only one that stays tense is the captain still above us near the wheelhouse.

"All righty then, greenhorn," as he unties the coffee cup and hands it to me. "Time to earn your bunk. Drink this and we'll call it square, yes, yes?!?!"

I look over the side of the boat while still holding the cup and the bubbles that were beside us have now trailed away behind us. "That's not a good idea, guys. I have no problem with most initiation efforts like this, and I know you guys don't know me that well. But drinking sea water is never a good idea, on top of dehydration and puking my lungs out. You can't tell me you all sat there and drank salt water for your rite of passage or whatever, did you?" I ask.

They all look at each other with smiles and shake their heads yes in unison. Even Comanche shakes his head yes, but doesn't speak like the rest of them do.

"Sure did..."

"Yep..."

"Me too..."

I lift the cup up and see several floaties in the sunlight and can smell the saltwater in my nostrils. "Do you guys make all the new guys do this? I mean... Come on guys. I'm just gonna end up barfing and then have to clean it all up myself."

"The last greenhorn refused to drink for the same thang you just said," says Scotty with a smile.

I look over to see Comanche and he raises his hand. I didn't notice his remarkably huge bowie knife in the other hand. He waves his knife in front of his raised hand, but drops his empty hand before he cuts himself. Just like the same gesture he did my first night on the boat and says the same thing again while shaking his head in contempt. "Hand... Gone..."

"Alright then guys... If this is what it takes."

They all come in closer in anticipation. Any closer, I might aim for them when I go to throw all this up. I look at the captain again and he now leans over the railing above us in the same level of anticipation. I close my eyes, preparing for the worst, and tilt the grungy coffee cup back. In the first gulp, I try to hold my breath at the same time. Then, the cold water goes down my throat. Not just any water. It's fresh water.

I pull the cup away from my mouth to take a closer look at it, and they all chuckle under their breath. They gave me a cup of fresh water. They must have switched it somehow, but I saw Scotty pull it directly from the ocean. I tilt it back again and empty the cup into my mouth. The cup was full of fresh water pulled from the ocean.

"It's fresh water," I say with a smile. "How'd you guys do that? Did you know it was fresh water?"

They all cheer and rush to pat me on the back and check shoulders all around. Comanche even joins in. As they all celebrate, I inspect the cup and turn it upside down to look for a false bottom, but it's just a normal old stained coffee cup. I look up at the captain and he just shake his head yes at me before quietly moving back into the wheelhouse.

"When did you switch it out?" I ask them.

"Naw, mate. You seen it with your own two eyes. Watched me yank it right out the ocean. Be no tricks here," Scotty answers. "Time for proper greetin's for the rest of the crew, yes," as he lights another cigarette.

Diesel reaches his long skinny black arm out, "Name's Diesel. Bona fide lover boy and porn star. You need your ol' lady filled with some sturdy boys, you hit me up when we get back to port."

"No, but is that why they call you Diesel?" I ask, while I reach back to shake his hand.

"No... It's mainly because I maintain the ship's engines and any other mechanical efforts they need when we ain't hauling in the nets. I'll take you down and show you around the engine bay before the end of the day."

"Alright then..."

Up next is Comanche with his massive hand. I won't miss this opportunity to stay on his good graces. Not after how we first met. He grabs my hand and shakes it hard enough to jolt my neck. "Hello again, Comanche... Glad we're on the same page now." He grunts with a smile before he lets go.

Beside Comanche is a slightly older man with a serious belly on him. His dark hair and beard all buzzed down to the same short length. Several years at sea have not been kind to his complexion. He reaches out his hand, "I'm the deck boss here. You'll see me operating the crane when we start reeling in. You need anything, you come to me. I'm the direct line of contact with the skipper and I tell you what to do. If I'm not around, then Scotty is your go to man," he says sternly. His grip doesn't seem as firm as the others, which can say a lot about a man. Either way, he doesn't care for my being here.

"And that's why we call him Deck Boss Dick," Scotty says, and the others laugh.

"That's Mr. Deck Boss Dick to you there, Scotsman. You're lucky I don't hit senior citizens when I'm sober, anyway."

"Ok then," as I smile with them.

Scotty grabs my attention to the last man in the group that hasn't said much. "This here's Iceman. 'Bout your age, give or take."

He is right at my height too, being the youngest of all of them. Most of his facial hair has yet to fully come in, as most of it seems to be unkempt on his neck. When he goes to say hello and shake my hand, his teeth are worse off than Diesel's set of "grill" type teeth. Iceman just has decaying crooked teeth. It all makes sense when he says, "Howdy…"

"Umm… Howdy to you too. Looks like we're the young guns here, Iceman. You're not from Massachusetts, are you?"

He lets go of my hand to lift his beanie and a mullet falls out from underneath as he scratches his scalp. "Nah, I'm from Florida."

"Yeah, he came from all them inbred swamp peoples down there, didn't ya hillbilly?" laughs Diesel and Scotty joins in the mockery.

I ignore their belittling of him.

"Gators, crawdads, snakes, bass, trout, and now some nor' Atlantic cod. If it lives and breathes in the water, I can catch it and put it on ice for ya. That's what I do when the haul comes in. You guys slice 'em up and I box them for the freezers on ice."

"Is that why they call you Iceman?" I ask.

"Oooh… Oooh. I got this one, Scotty," says Diesel. He wraps his arm on top of the short stature of Iceman. "This hillbilly here we call Iceman because his first winter season out as a greenhorn, he felt the need to get his foot caught in the net as we dropped it in, and he went in with it! Water was so cold that year, when we pulled him back up, he was a dammed ol' block of ice."

Iceman just agrees and shakes his head at the elaborate tale of how he got his sea name.

Scotty goes to run his mouth again. I didn't know the Scottish like to hear the sound of their own voice so much. "We had to chisel the ice off his nip-ons, his fingers and toes, even his damn ass cheeks were frozen together."

"And here's the best part," says Diesel, coming back into the conversation. "That water was so cold that his lil' dick is now forever frozen solid as a rock." He raises up his pinky and wiggles the top of it in Iceman's face.

"That's bullshit, Diesel, and you know it," Iceman says in disgust as he slaps Diesel's hand away. "Least I'm not the bona fide sex offender."

"Hey… That's some low blow there, hillbilly. She was seventeen and a half and you know it. Said so on her ID. You just mad ya lil' frozen pecker didn't get all up in that," he says, while making several thrusting motions against Iceman's hips in a sexual gesture. Iceman just laughs and pushes him away.

A smaller phone near the crane control rings, and Dick walks over to answer it. The crew disperses from their huddle, leaving me with just Scotty again.

"Skipper says chow and bed down within two hours, ya bunch of schoolgirls. First net gets dropped in the AM. Get your shit done!"

I hand the empty coffee cup back to Scotty before he walks away too. "Hey… You already had drinking water in that cup right?"

"No there, matey. You saw me pull that cup up from the side of the boat full of ocean water, just like everyone else did. No tricks here."

"I'm so lost?"

"But that's what we come out here for there, Yankee." He leans in closer. "Some be runnin' from somethin'. Some come to find somethin'. Either way, we all come out here to get lost. Ya' see. There's an entire ocean out there. The land folk seem to forget the ocean covers most of the world. In all reality, it is her world and we're just fishin' in it. And boy, is she full of mystery. You drank from a freshwater spout in the middle of the ocean. How many land folk say they would believe you if you told them? We have to trust each other 'cause we depend on each other out here. So, one of us tells you to do somethin', best you trust us that we know what we're doing."

"Trust?"

"That be right, greenhorn. Trust. Because out here, we are all we got. Out here, the impossible can become possible. Without trust, that big blue ocean will swallow you up. She can be your best friend, or your worst enemy, because that big blue mysterious unknown will gladly scare you if you let her."

He pats me on the back with a smile, but more serious than he's ever been the last few days. I take another long look at the blue horizon before the engine revs up, then it dawns on me to ask him before he walks below.

"Hey Scotty…" He turns back to me while in the doorway. "What happened to the last greenhorn with you guys? Couldn't get a straight answer out of Comanche the other night." He turns to look at Dick, still messing with the crane and winch cables near the control cluster. Dick just glares back at us both as Scotty thinks about how to answer that one.

Then Scotty answers, "Coast Guard had to come chopper him out mid trip."

"Why?" Scotty just looks back at Dick, but he ignores us and turns his back to look busy with something else.

"Got his hand caught in the pulley system bringing in one of the nets. A massive freak wave came in and ripped his hand right off his arm before we could get him untangled. Lost his hand in the water, and they had to chopper him out. He's lucky to be alive. That net weighs in at several hundred pounds when it comes in full and those cables can rip you in half if you're standing in the wrong place at the wrong time."

I swallow my heart back down into my chest as he walks closer. Comanche really wasn't lying. The last greenhorn's hand was cut off in the cables.

Scotty puts his hand back on my shoulder, "Remember, Greenhorn, we gotta trust to have each other's backs out here. This is her world, not ours. And we're just fishin' in it."

Chapter 6 - Wayfaring Stranger

Yellow Jack cooked us up a Hispanic slop with some grizzled taco meat and most of us aren't fans of it. Not that he hangs around in the mess area to hear our gripes and opinions. He makes his and the captain's plate and returns to the wheelhouse. Comanche doesn't even stick around for the meal we all force ourselves to eat. The rest of the crew all leave a mess for me to clean up as the greenhorn. They chat it up with several hands of cards while they all gripe their contentions over Yellow Jack, his freeloading ways, and horrible cooking efforts. None of them seem to like him and he has tagged along with the crew several times over the last few seasons, but nobody knows his story. The captain keeps Yellow Jack with him in the wheelhouse until he catches a ride elsewhere at some point when we reach the fishing grounds. I stay out of the conversations as I scrub dishes and cookware, just listening to understand the crew's mindset better and keep feeding them fresh coffee as I clean.

The port holes on the side of the ship near the kitchen area grow dark and frosty on the outside, but the ship glides along gently, without a single toss or turn in the last few hours. They all bundle up in sweaters and beanie caps as the cold sets in, but they keep laughing with old sea tales, playing cards, chugging the coffee, and smoking up the entire room with their cigarettes.

"I'm tellin' ya, ya Yank bloats," Scotty elaborates his tale. "I had this one beauty in the Royal Navy, back before I came to the states. She had the biggest tightest snare drum ass ya' ever saw. Never saw one like it since... Not in the states, anyway." Motioning his hands on how big her backside was.

"Oh, yeah...?" Iceman says with a smile as he tries to focus on his hand of cards.

"Did you catch *HIS* name before or after you gave it to him in the rear?" asks Diesel sarcastically.

Dick spits his coffee out as they laugh together. "Sounds like you and him had a good ol' time back in the day there, Scotty. I'll be sleeping on my backside tonight if that's the way ya swing."

I finish up my duties as the new guy and try to scurry out of the smoke-filled mess.

"Be sure all that shit's put away, Greenhorn. No time to be cleanin' up after you when the nets start coming in," says Dick.

"Already did, sir…"

"Leave 'em alone, Dick. He's put in his share," says Scotty as he gives me a wink. "Get some sleep, kid. Unless you wanna play a hand with all us losers."

"You guys are the ones losin'. Not me. If we were playin' for money, I'd be rich off you idiots by now," Iceman says.

"No thanks guys. I think I'll catch some fresh air and turn in before the real fun begins."

They don't seem to give me, the greenhorn, another thought as I walk away. I can hear them laughing and cracking more jokes at each other as far as the sleeping quarters. Comanche's curtain is already closed for his bunk, so I keep the noise down to not wake him. I lift the mattress and grab the violin case and a few extra sweaters to put on over me. I glimpse at myself in the tiny handheld mirror attached on the end of the bunk. I haven't shaved since I got on the bus to leave the base. Other than my pearly whites that I have been overprotective of since I could remember, I'm starting to look like the rest of these guys. Disheveled and unkempt. I cover my ears with my beanie cap and head up from below deck.

The skies are clear and starry, with a cold that hasn't hit this deep in a while. Every star in the sky is as bright as can be, and my nostrils try to freeze up while I look around. Little to no lights on deck, except for the low dim coming from the wheelhouse above me. I just look around and listen as the small ripples lead away from us as the boat trudges on further and further from home. Streetlights and passing cars would never allow a view like this with no cloud in the sky. The moon is hidden behind us somewhere, but still close enough to give every star its own level of intensity. Hundreds of miles away from all civilization is what it takes to feel the most alive. Lost in all my overwhelmed sensory of the Atlantic, with no one waiting for my return with warm embrace and a decent meal, but I feel more at home than I have in a long time.

I find a spot to sit near the barrels with the stockpile of netting on my backside to block the frigid breeze. I haven't played this thing in a while and hopefully it's not too far out of tune. I made sure I didn't leave this behind in our small apartment near the base, just for her to ruin too. She never cared for it or hearing me play. Said no matter the type of tune I made, it always sounded sad. Well, the hell with her. I like the sound of its calmness. The calmness, like the sea is on a serene night like this is. So calm there is almost no line for a horizon where the stars meet the sea. The only noise is the low rumble of the engines that push us forward into a welcoming black void of open ocean.

The bow is a used replacement from a few years ago when the original was broken during shipping. The fresh case with red velvet interior keeps the entire piece safe and sound and to prevent that from happening again. The chin rest scrubs against my facial hair stubble from the last few days and I look around before I commit to playing a chord to make sure I'm alone. The first few strokes screech loud enough to shatter windows. I adjust the tuning pegs to bring it back in sync. I hope nobody heard that first attempt in more than several months.

A few deep breaths to lower my heart rate and tension. Don't hold it too hard on the neck or chin. I place my fingers in the right spot and tell myself it's like riding a bicycle. Movements are made with the elbow. But to play any instrument, to really play, it's not about making the right noise. It's about feeling more than what you're hearing. I close my eyes and hit the D string just right. It sounds a bit deeper than I remember, but it may need more tuning. I only wish my mother knew I still played, and all her bought lessons for me after school were not a waste. Now, there is nobody here to judge me, only the open skies and ocean to hear the music I play.

I keep playing the violin with my eyes closed, and my fingers and elbows do all the work for me. The music comes in as an old folk tune, *Wayfaring Stranger*.

It's a gospel type tune from the southern regions, but it is one of the first tunes I learned to play when I started, mainly because it is not expected to be played very fast. Just slowly and smoothly is the trick. The sound of the boat engine disappears. I know I'm still on the open ocean but have forgotten I am on a fishing trawler. The sounds of each string and cord change echoes louder throughout the ocean.

I play it for several minutes, not that I was keeping track of how long I was playing. Then the ocean replies in the form of a splash nearby. That was no wave breaching on the side of the ship. It was too sudden, but not close enough either. I keep playing with my eyes closed, remembering brighter days. Another splash happens that closes in the distance from the first one that I heard. That's when I hear them. That's when I hear something else playing a tune with me. That's when I hear a whale song.

I stroke a few more chords, with no particular tune in mind. Just trying to respond to them as they come to the surface for air in their blow holes. I can't see any of them in the darkness, just the water that they blow out faintly across the starry horizon. I wish I had my phone to record this, but maybe it's best to keep this one moment for me. A few more tunes, and they sing back with their moans and sounds repeatedly. I've heard them on sonar devices on the aircraft carriers before, but never like this in the open ocean. They attempt to make a similar sounding reply to each chord I play. There must be an entire family of whales out there. If they even travel as a family.

The flick of a lighter on the deck grabs my attention. I lower my violin to look around to see who's up here with me, while the whales keep singing. Another flick of a lighter and I see Comanche sitting on the bottom of the steps that lead up to the wheelhouse. Covered in a thick blanket and smoking his pipe again.

"Jesus Comanche… Have you been sitting there the entire time?"

He takes a long puff of his pipe, and saying nothing, he just shakes his head yes.

I feel embarrassed for a moment, then I remember he doesn't speak enough broken English to tell the others what I was doing up here alone. Even though it's nothing to frown on, I don't see any of these crusty sea hooligans appreciating the sound of a violin. I reach for my case to put it away.

"No," Comanche says, as he raises his hand. "Good music… Sing with them," as he points toward the sea. I'm guessing, he wants to hear the whales responding to the sounds of hitting single chords again. I kinda do too.

I slowly move my bow across the strings, making the same tune as the song I was playing before. Another whale breaches and sings in the distance as I play along from memory.

"She calls for you…" Comanche says during a pause between chord changes. I think I get it now, because the captain said the same thing. He looks out toward the whales and their sounds and splashes start to fade away behind us. I lower my violin, knowing the rumble of the engines may fade out my violin for the whales as they move in the opposite direction of us. My violin case gets closed up and we keep listening to them as they move further and further away and Comanche quietly sits there, smoking his long pipe.

"Do you think those were Orca whales, maybe?"

He shakes his head no between puffs and says, "Humpback."

I walk over closer to Comanche and look over the side of the ship, but the cluster of whales are behind us now, still splashing and singing in the distance.

"Like birds," he says.

"What do you mean?"

He points behind the ship, holding the pipe with the other hand close to his mouth. "Like birds… South for winter… North for summer."

"Right. I didn't know that. I've never been this close to them, much less play a tune with them."

Comanche just agrees with me with a faint smile. He reaches his arm out with his pipe, assuming to offer me a smoke of it.

"Oh… No thanks. I probably smoke too much as is. But I'm not as bad as the rest of the guys, apparently."

He goes back to smoking his pipe and I zip up my jacket to break away from the cold northern breeze that blasts us on the deck. Comanche is not even phased by the icy chill in the air, it seems. I question if he was ever the type to be concerned with any form of threat or danger. Not just from his sheer size and strength, but his demeanor alone.

"Seems odd, doesn't it?" I ask him. He just looks at me, puzzled. "All the ocean life seems to head south to warmer waters for the season. All the while we, the intelligent human species, head north into the cold and ruthless gray waters of the winter season."

He looks at me, confused again, shaking his head, not understanding.

"They call that irony… Or a coincidence, maybe. Do you understand this word? Irony?"

He just laughs lightly under his breath and shakes his head as he looks away from me and out to sea again. He turns back and reaches out his pipe to offer it to me again.

"Irony," he says, while still reaching his pipe out to me.

"Right… Ok, then Comanche." I take him up on his offer of smoking his pipe.

I sit down on the step below him and he motions his hands on how to hold it and smoke it. I take in a deep drag and begin coughing immediately. He chuckles under his breath again and slaps me hard on the back a few times to help clear my lungs. After I catch my breath, he motions again how to properly smoke his pipe in his turn to take a drag. He hands it back to me, and I am more careful this time not to treat it like a cigarette. The same response happened to me the last time I tried a cigar on a ship. Took it in like a cigarette and my fellow seamen said my face turned green as grass.

"Irony…" he says, with his deep voice and obvious sarcasm this time.

"Right. You definitely know more English than you let on, don't you?"

He takes a turn with his pipe and ignores my question by looking out to sea and listening to the fading whale songs.

"You know, all those months out on the navel aircraft carries, it never felt like I was really out here, ya know?" He just gives me another familiar puzzled look. "Yeah… It was like this massive steel city that just hovers around in the ocean, ya know? It was like the further away from home we got, the more they tried to function as if we were still at home." He hands me the pipe to take a smoke as I keep talking. "Shops. Indoor running tracks. Theaters. Ice cream parties… It never made sense to me to live like that when we were out at sea." I hand his pipe back to him after blowing the smoke away from him. "Working in the Med Bay on the ship, dealing with colds and broken nails, it's like we rarely even got to see the ocean. But all most of us would want is someone to come home to, but most of us were invisible to them."

"Women…" he says, handing his pipe back to me. I've lost count of how many times he's handed his pipe back to me and I still don't know what I'm smoking with him. I'd rather not know.

"Right… Women. I remember. What about you Comanche? What's your story? A woman at home waiting for you?"

He just keeps a stern look out towards the sea without answering me. "Well, I used to… Gone now, but I did at one point. She seems like forever ago somehow now." I go to hand the pipe back to him.

He motions me to keep smoking. "Smoke more…"

I look up at him and he just takes a deep breath in. Like life and relaxation fills his lungs. Or maybe it's whatever we are smoking here on the deck.

"She calls to you."

"What do you mean?" I ask him.

He points at the whales that are still singing in the fading distance behind us. "She sings to you… Now, smoke more… Talk less…"

I shake my head yes as we keep passing the pipe back and forth. We listen quietly and intently until we can hear the whale song no more in the distance.

All that remains are the stars in the invisible horizon line above the ocean water.

Light splashes slap against the hull of the ship as we steam further and further away.

Further away from the world we knew and deeper into the frigid night.

Chapter 7 - The Grand Banks

The boat is getting tossed around more and more the further north we go, not to mention how much colder it is getting. It doesn't take too many men to drop the net, but as a greenhorn, I get the least amount of sleep. Mainly because my duties aren't as detailed or technical as most of the others. Dick and I are the only ones up for now. I just follow along with whatever he says to do. The massive trawl doors of the ship open and lead out to the sea behind us while saltwater splashes the side of the ship in the dark hours of the morning. Air so cold I struggle to take a breath as I tirelessly muscle and guide the net out into the water. He lowers the net in with the winch, and I just guide it as it drags off the boat when dropping down into the water. The more of the net that goes in, the weight of it helps it get dragged down into the depths faster and faster. I can see how Iceman was dragged in with the net as a greenhorn.

Deck Boss Dick has me right at the boat's edge. However, he would just have to turn away for one second and a loose knot could drag me down into the sea with it. Then no one would ever know.

He watches me closely from behind the winch and crane controls. My feet slip around in my boots filled with water and I keep a grip on anything I can reach as I walk around. I look up to see Yellow Jack and Skipper Walsh watching both of us. Skipper points the spotlight at me as the net continues to drop into the water. Lastly, the otter anchors go in. They stay mounted to the side of the ship near the rear trawl doors until most of the net is in. The otter anchors are really just a pair of heavy weights that look like an anchor with a specific shape that keeps the net opened as wide as possible on each side while under the water's surface. I just stay out of the way for this, as the weight of the net drags them across the deck. Once the otter anchors are down in the water with the net, the net and otter anchor rig travels along underwater wide open to catch anything in its path. The engine RPMs grow louder once the otter anchors are down. I watch the remaining steel cables spread apart, showing us that the nets are widening out under the surface. Dick calls up the skipper from the deck phone saying the net is in and the spotlight on me goes dark, along with the rest of the deck.

"We can drag for two hours max out here this time of year. Try to get some sleep, Greenhorn," says Dick.

We both head back below, but sleep may be out of the question from my anticipation. I climb into my bunk after hanging my rain gear and everyone sleeps quietly, beyond the few that snore. I just lay there listening to the engine RPMs struggle more and more to pull the weight of a filling net. The ship gets battered around by the sea. I hear various smaller items around the bunk room and kitchen get tossed to the floor. We feel every ripple, every splash, and every wave from the ocean. These guys just sleep soundly through it all, though. I tell myself I've been spoiled from being on much larger hunks of steel in the ocean in recent months. So, a large rogue wave feels more like taking on a speed bump too fast in your car. In this boat, in this frigid weather on choppy seas, everything is felt tenfold.

I close my eyes and wait, hoping to actually fall asleep, but it's just not gonna happen for me. Not this close to sunrise. I keep checking my watch and try to get lost in my thoughts. The sun will make an appearance when the first net gets pulled in. Then it will be a nonstop revolving effort. Net comes in, fish off the deck, net goes back out for two hours, and that's the time slot we have to process, pack, and store the catch in the freezer. A lot of moving parts and I dread the idea of a cluster of disgruntled seamen, more experienced than me, hating me for not knowing what I'm up against. My anxiety doesn't even let me keep my eyes closed. I look around at the graffiti and cigarette burns under the bunk above me. Two hours doesn't seem to go by fast enough right now.

The rocking boat's engine RPMs rev high, but we slow down at the same time. The sound of a strumming electric guitar and keyboard comes through the loudspeaker system. The music is everywhere blasting my eardrums and the rest of the crew gets up in a frenzy.

"Put ya lil' dick beaters away there mate and let's go catch some damn fish, Greenhorn," yells Scotty, as he thrusts the curtain open.

They all bump into each other as they scurry around looking for their boots and gear. I jump out of bed and do the same. I get my gear on before most of them. They all wear orange, Dick wears red, and I wear green. I put my waterproof beanie on and head up.

"All hands-on deck... All hands-on deck!!! Get up here ASAP, you buncha' shitheads. We're pullin' heavy!!!" Skipper Walsh's voice comes booming over the music in the loudspeakers.

Comanche is already making his way up to the deck. I assume everyone stays out of his way to not get trampled on like a herd of buffalo coming at you. Scotty turns around as I slip my boots on and hands me a fillet knife still in the sheath.

"We gotta slice them open to bleed out before we send them down the chute."

I shake my head yes and we all sprint up the steps that lead to the deck. I run by a small loudspeaker and that's when I think I recognize the classic rock.

"Are we listening to *Styx?*" I ask Iceman, right in front of me.

"Hell yeah! *Blue Collar Man*…When the 70s and 80s come on in the tunes, that means the Skip is happy 'cause the net is heavy. Nuttin' beats slavin' away to some good ol' fashin' classic rock, bro!"

The icy winds are brutal. Even more harsh than they were a few hours ago when the net went down. All men rush to the deck. The rocking ship and the water that splashes around us doesn't even faze them, as they run to their respective positions near the trawl doors at the back of the ship. Like children headed to the tree on Christmas morning, they all wait anxiously when Deck Boss Dick heads over to the crane and winch operating controls. Scotty keeps me close and I keep at least one hand on any railing I can find just to not be thrown overboard. All the others have their sea legs about them, focused and waiting for the otter anchors to come in first. Scotty has me stay away for this part, as the massive otter anchors come in at several hundred pounds. Scotty and I bring in the ropes to stow away, while the others muscle the otter anchors in place and secure them with chains on the side of the ship. They rely on Comanche to hold each one in place, against the freezing waves and tilting ship, while Iceman and Diesel bolt them down to the side of the ship. This keeps them ready for when the net goes right back in after being emptied.

Then we wait as Dick winches in the net. Nobody can be in the way of that cable, and I don't plan on losing a hand like the last greenhorn. The crew is quiet. Very quiet. The spotlight from the wheelhouse is turned on and hovers around all of us before pointing at the trawl door opening at the end of the ship. I look up to see the skipper and Yellow Jack, just as eager as the rest of the crew.

Scotty hands over his pack of cigarettes and says, "Pop a fag, aye?" Everyone seems to smoke as they wait patiently. The deck is quiet with the exception of the winch that is struggling to pull in the net. The sea rages all around us, and I can barely hang on. But everyone stays focused on that cable as it slowly reels in the catch, if any catch at all. The skipper shuts down the engine as the steel cables reveal the end of the netting. Scotty notices me looking at him puzzled, wondering why the engine was shut down.

"Only temporary. He'll do that, so the net doesn't get caught in the propellor," Scotty yells in my ear over the water that splashes in.

"Will they kill all the engines when the net goes back out empty too!?!?"

"It depends," as he takes another puff of his cigarette. "If the current is against you, it won't bother it none!" He holds a finger up to motion me to be quiet. I shake my head and watch out the trawl doors of the ship with the others. Nobody moves. Nobody says anything to each other. We stand like statues braving the harsh weather and ocean around us without a single flinch or shiver from the cold. These men have never been this quiet. The ship has never created an atmosphere of such tension on a comparable scale since I boarded. Absolute focus and esteemed concentration on the cables that the winch brings in. We forget what crews like this are willing to endure to bring in the big catch. The labor. The exhaustion. The danger of the high seas. All in the name of making a dollar and put food on a stranger's plate. But it all becomes well worth it for them. When that first cluster of fish is seen caught in the net, Scotty just turns to tap my shoulder and smile. The winch struggles more as the rest of the net is dragged in and reveals a full catch with several hundred fish, squirming and gasping for their last breath of life.

"Oh yeah!!!" yells Diesel, waving his hands in the air.

Comanche and Iceman high five as more water is splashed on them.

"Look at that, Greenhorn!!!" Scotty yells back at me, excited as can be.

I smile with them. It is more than a paycheck caught in those nets. It is a lifestyle that I had forgotten about, since shipping from one port to the next in the Navy. It is the simplest form of life for these men. Me too now, maybe. Reeling in the big catch, with nobody but the sea to thank for it.

Loads of fish start to fall out on the deck, but Scotty has me hold in place while the winch on the crane lifts up the net to get the end of it just above the deck. The net is almost fully suspended in the air and overflowing with cod fish of all sorts.

"Close the rear trawl door and tables out," yells Dick from behind the crane controls.

Diesel brings in the trawl doors they dragged the net through, while Iceman uses a large metal pole with a special hook on it to lift another hatch open on the deck. They are raised up like a platform with walls on all four sides. The center of the table is slightly raised too, but with an opening only large enough for a fish to be thrown down into the slaughterhouse for further processing before going into the freezers. They hurry as the net that hangs above sways with the tossing ship.

"*Get that net emptied!!!*" Skipper Walsh yells at us through the loudspeaker.

Scotty grabs my arm and we run to the bottom of the net too. Dick lowers the winch so Scotty can reach the pull string. I grab the pull string on the other side and mounds of fish fall down to our feet, flapping around all over the deck. We all work together, shaking the net to get every fish out and toss them on the deck. There are so many moving pieces with such a small crew, but everyone has their jobs and I just try to keep up. Comanche grabs the now empty net to be readied for the next drop as he hand-motions to Dick which way he was moving with the net. Iceman runs around the deck with a wide squeegee type broom to sweep all the fish to the center near the raised platform used as a table. The classic rock music comes blasting over the speakers again. Diesel grabs a random cod off the deck and sings to it like a microphone in his hand. He sings along to the music while a fish is wiggling in one hand and a knife in the other.

"*That's a good haul, boys and girls! Bleed em' and clean em' down below,*" says the skipper through the loudspeaker.

Scotty keeps me close and we pull out our fillet knives.

"Ya grab one! Ya slit the artery underneath," he says while grabbing a fish to hold it upside down and shows me. "Right there between the gills. There, ya see!" as he slices it open. Then he throws it to the center of the table to fall down into the chute that leads below deck to the slaughterhouse. "That's so they bleed out and die before we get down to the cleanin' room for packin'! Just don't cut yourself, aye?!"

I start bleeding out fish as fast as I can and throw them down the chute in the middle of the table. Iceman now uses a snow shovel to scoop them up onto the table. Soon enough, the others join in on the bleeding efforts. Even with several hundred fish all over the deck, we get them cut open to bleed out in no time. I prick my hand a few times with the sharp fillet knife, but my thick rubber gloves take the grunt of the cut for me. Dick makes a count of all fish going on the table for weight and calls it up to the skipper through his phone near the crane controls. Comanche, Scotty, Diesel, and I slice the fish open as fast as we can. When Iceman shovels in the last few fish on top of the weight table, he joins in the effort.

Once the last fish is thrown in to bleed out, the table platform is lowered, and the deck is reset to send the net back out again. Dick takes his place behind the crane controls. The guys start to muscle around with the otter anchors again to have them ready to send back down. Scotty runs over to open the rear trawl doors on the backside of the boat, just as a rogue wave splashes down over the deck, sending me sliding on my belly towards the wheelhouse steps. Saltwater and fish blood fill my mouth, but I get back up in a hurry. The skipper points his spotlight at me, and I give him the thumbs up that I'm ok.

The net quickly follows behind out into the water. Comanche and Diesel get the otter anchors loose and then they slam down into the water too. Once the net is far enough away, the engines are started back up to better steer the ship. With weather like this, Scotty tells me not to worry about cleaning off the deck. Most of the fish blood has washed away already with the last wave that slammed us on the back of the ship. I help Scotty stow away any loose gear, and we all make our way down below.

"Now the real fun begins," he says with a smile, as he closes the door leading to the deck. "Down grade your gear to dry off then head to the slaughterhouse. Keep your gloves and hat on."

Dick is already in the tiny cleaning room next to the massive load of fish, writing numbers and looking at more weight scales. How he gets a proper number and weight of all the fish that comes in during all that chaos beats the hell outta me, but he maintains communications with the skipper in the wheelhouse with the various phones throughout the ship. Iceman lays out freshly sharpened knives of all sorts at each station, then moves to organize some plastic wrapping at the end of the table made of butcher block. There's four of us, two on each side of the table, and we have various buckets behind us. Then Scotty explains everything to me.

"When this starts, it happens as quickly as possible. We got two hours to clean them before the next net comes up. Iceman sprays, disinfects, and dollies each box we fill to the freezer. We take turns here on the line who's cutting what, but it's the same efforts on each side. We grab the fish, first we cut the heads, then the tail, then we gut them out last. No piece is wasted. You find a fish still breathing, cut it again to bleed out and set it aside 'til it's dead. The buckets behind you are for all the various extra pieces, like the head, tails, and guts. Iceman will box them up and freeze them too once they're filled up, but they don't fill as fast. The faster we get this done, the longer we get to rest before the next net gets wheeled in. By the time this part is done with, you'll want to go back out on deck for some fresh air, no matter how bad the weather is out there."

They all laugh while they take their stations. I guess Dick is just, kinda, overseeing things? Maybe? He doesn't do much. The deck boss's laziness leaves my mind when the assembly line effort of fish processing begins. The smell is blood curdling to my stomach about half an hour in. I've never been one to get seasick or motion sickness, but the smell has no place to escape this small slaughterhouse below deck. I cover my nose and swallow vomit back down my throat, but they can all see my face turning green.

Dick makes his way out of the slaughterhouse, but not without a few cross words towards me. "If you're gonna puke, Greenhorn, then make sure it lands in one of the gut buckets behind you and not on the cleanin' table. Fuckin' pussy," he says, and slams the door behind him.

They all look at me as I keep trying to cut and clean every fish that heads my way. Diesel turns on some more classic rock tunes through a radio nearby connected to a dusty old MP3 player. We all keep working and I finally let loose a vomit that can't be held back anymore.

"Don't worry 'bout him, Greenhorn. You'll get used to it a few nets in." Scotty assures me while they all laugh at me puking my brains out.

"Yeah... that's why we call him Dick, and even he knows it," says Iceman, as he walks around us with crates of processed fish on the dolly.

I lift my head back up from the gut bucket and shake it off.

"Yeah… He just gonna run up to kiss the skipper's ass while we down here doing all the work and make him look good," says Diesel. "He up there all the time, puckerin' them lips up for the Captain… Like this," and he pushes out his lips to Comanche standing right next to him. Diesel acts like he's about to kiss him, but Comanche lifts his knife and points it at him before he has the chance to lean in closer to him. Diesel backs off in a hurry and goes back to cleaning fish, even though the rest of us lightly laugh at them both.

"So… Are we like all alone now?" Iceman winks at us, as he comes back with an empty dolly.

Diesel and Scotty just look at each other with a childish grin and shake their head yes.

"Go get the real diesel we need, Iceman," Scotty tells him. "Looks like the newbie here could use some too."

I try to catch my breath and shake off the smell to prevent another dry heave of vomit. But it's no use. With very little ventilation down here, it feels like the walls are closing in with the smell of festering fish guts and cigarette smoke. Iceman comes back with some water bottles, but they are not filled with water. They are filled with some sort of darker liquid that looks thick enough to be oil. Iceman hands each of us one and Scotty doesn't wait around to open his up and take a drink.

"Ahhh… Yes… Now that's some good stuff there, aye mates?"

"Leave it to the hillbilly to make the good stuff," says Diesel.

I lift the bottle up to look at it closely, in all its dark spit filled looking nastiness and glory. "What the hell is this stuff?"

"It's a bit of dark soda mixed in with several loads of my own skeet skeet skeet… That'll warm ya up there, Greenhorn."

Scotty and Iceman, who's already drinking from his bottle too, laugh at Diesel's sick joke. I look at Comanche and he just shakes his head no in disgust as he keeps cleaning fish.

"It's some of my own lager type beer. Toilet bowl grog like, and I made it myself," says Iceman. "Take a sip and tell me what ya think."

"Are we allowed to have this onboard?"

"This ain't the Navy, Greenhorn. And it'll keep ya warm and steady when we head back up to bring in the next net. I keep it stashed in one of the empty oil barrels. Nobody needs to know how we keep going out here. As long as we come home with the catch, they don't ask."

Even Comanche shakes his head yes in agreeing. At this point, I'll try anything to help keep the vomit down and to lose focus on the smell in here. I open the bottle and do as he asks. It goes down like syrup, almost.

But I can taste the alcohol embedded in it. I light up a cigarette as we keep working. They all laugh and Scotty slaps me on the back in praise. If you can't beat them, I guess just join them. Not that I was trying to compete with them. I'm only competing with the stench in this room by covering the smell of dead fish with all our combined dark beer burbs and taco farts layered in with all the cigarette smoke. Eventually, during our laughter and sing along efforts with whatever classic rock is playing, everyone forgets how bad the smell of gutted fish is. We lose track of time cleaning fish and getting tipsy on Iceman's homemade toilet bowl grog. That's the routineness of this job most think they could never do when things are going smoothly on a commercial fishing ship, according to the guys anyway.

We bring the nets in.

Empty the nets.

And send the nets back out.

Bleed the fish on deck.

Clean the fish and pack them away.

Do it all over again every two hours.

And somehow… We stay shit-faced drunk the entire time just to stay warm and awake…

Chapter 8 - The Mule

It goes on like this for three days. Maybe four? I lost track of time. Sometimes the seas are fair and calm, but most of the time they are choppy and frigid. The occasional overcast that allows very little blue sky to come through gives us the indicator that another day has passed. That's the only time that I can think of that the ocean becomes blue again. Beyond that, the seas remain dark, gray, and angry just by our very presence here. The crew keeps their spirits up with lighthearted jokes and details of prior sexcapades with women back home. When the net comes in, it's usually heavy and full. Occasionally, we'll get a welcomed light catch that we can process fast and catch an extra few minutes of sleep. It seems as soon as we lay our heads down, the horns and classic rock music on the loudspeaker wakes us all up again. I catch a glimpse of myself in the mirror again when dawning my wet gear and hat. Both eyes are red, and my shadow has turned into a full-on beard. Teeth remain stained with cheap coffee no matter how hard I brush them between nets. We have no one to impress with our looks out here. And when that net comes in full, the excitement makes the concerns of little things go away for all of us.

We rarely see the skipper, and even less of Yellow Jack. He'll cook some variation of slop for us while we're busy on deck or down below so that we can eat before bed down. I ask the rest of the crew about him often and what his purpose is here. Why he never helps, beyond light kitchen duties? Especially when we have a large haul that comes in with the net. An extra hand would make things go by quicker to assist in more sleep. But even Dick seems below Yellow Jack in his duties, according to the skipper. Everyone has the same opinion about Yellow Jack. A dead head, they call him. A free ride to a turning point in the journey, orchestrated by the skipper somehow. One day he is with the ship, the next day he is gone.

Yellow Jack has tagged along like this for the last few seasons, apparently. Then he gets off with another boat to push into Canada, sometimes a bigger or smaller boat. Either way, nobody likes him or trusts him. Not because he mainly speaks Spanish. But how the skipper keeps him well guarded and babied with him in the wheelhouse, no matter how much the crew may need an extra hand on deck or below. Not my place as the greenhorn to have my opinion heard, but I can definitely agree with them on that. Any abled body available, if only in the effort of all of us getting more sleep, should jump at the opportunity. At this point, I don't think the rest of us would want his help out of spite and contempt.

We have a streak of sunlight for the first time in a while. I can hear the winch and cables pulling hard and struggling with yet another heavy load. We all celebrate each time we get one this big to come in. Even Comanche smiles in his stone-cold tattooed face when he sees the amount of fish that gets dropped on the deck. Deck Boss Dick earns his name's sake though. It becomes obvious the longer we're out here how he earned his name. Any excuse to be a jerk to the others is taken on his part. Most of the others ignore him now with their time on the ship and the experience gained. Which makes me the easy target for Dick to make a verbal jab any time he can.

"Keep your fuckin' hands off that cable, Greenhorn!!!" Dick yells. I move to grab the railing and other ropes nearby, just to keep my footing.

The skipper comes out as we're bleeding out all the fish, several of which are still flapping around on the deck, attempting to make an escape off the side of the ship and avoid Iceman's snow shovel. Skipper

Walsh watches us for a bit before he speaks up. "Eight hour shut down boys. No nets down for a while. Time for some area beautification before catching up on sleep and grub. Make sure it happens, Dick."

"Gotchya, Skip," says Dick from underneath the wheelhouse.

Then the skipper returns to the wheelhouse without another word.

"You heard him, boys. Let's get this haul bled and gutted. Then we get a break after some custodian services are done," he says, laughing.

We all get another wind of energy in us and the sunlight, that has been a rarity the last few days, definitely helps things go faster. We drop the bleeding cod fish down into the funnel at the center of the table faster, with all us working on double time.

"What's area beautification? As if I don't already know…" I ask.

"Didn't swab enough poop-decks in the Navy there, Greenhorn?" Diesel laughs with a cigarette in his mouth.

"Nah, mate. He don't look the type to be servicin' the back door of my fair lady land whales to clean out the packed fudge like you do, Diesel." Scotty says in sarcasm.

"Oh... Oh... Scotsman's got jokes, does he? You da one love gettin' that back door cleaned out. Pop another fag then. Wouldn't be your first time."

Iceman keeps shoveling fish on the table as fast as he can while we all laugh and he answers me, "We have to sanitize the entire processing area where we clean the fish."

I look at Comanche bleeding fish with the rest of us and he shakes his head yes. "Pine trees," he says.

"Pine trees?" I ask. "What do you mean?"

"Pines trees," says Diesel, mocking Comanche's deep, low voice. "He means we use Pine Sol to clean the processing room, stupid. When you gonna learn some proper English. Get some damn audio tapes or somethin' bro. Guess it reminds him of livin' in the teepee back home. Too dumb to learn more than a few words at a time, tribal boy?"

Comanche just tries to ignore Diesel's attempt to ridicule him. He really pushes his luck with the big guy and it finally gets to him. As soon as Diesel bends over beside him to pick up a handful of fish, Comanche grabs a smaller fish still flopping around on the table and drops it down Diesel's raincoat. Scotty and I just watch the show about to begin while Comanche goes back to work as if nothing happened.

"Ahhh!!!... What the fu..." He starts jumping and hopping around on the deck, waving his knife around in one hand and throws his cigarette over the side of the ship with the other hand. He reaches around inside his coat and trips over Iceman's snow shovel and spills all the fish he had on it before he can unload it onto the table.

"Dammit, Diesel!!! What the hell's wrong with you?!?!" Iceman yells, trying to get the fish back on his shovel.

"There's somethin' in my coat! There's somethin' in my coat! Shit… It's flopping around down in my pants!"

We watch and laugh as Diesel takes a boot off, hops around on one foot on the deck, and squirms one pant leg around as the tiny fish finally falls out. Even Dick watches the show and bends over laughing in Diesel's moment of distress over a fish, now flipping around on the deck. It might be an epic three or four inches long.

"We're lucky there, mate," Scotty says. "Bigger ships that have the assembly lines for processing the fish. They have to sanitize every two days. We be a bit smaller, so it's only 'bout once a week for us here."

Once the goofing around is done on deck, our work goes faster. We head down to the cleaning room and slice these fish up for packaging in record time. How we pulled that off with a few hours of sleep spanned across several days beats the hell outta me.

Iceman hauls away the last cluster of cleaned out fish and the scraps that came from them in a hurry. Comanche disappears for a bit and comes back with a box of sanitization cleaner, paper towels, bleach, and, of course, his beloved Pine Sol. Dick does what Dick does best during area beautification of the slaughterhouse, as little work as possible, but as much delegating as he can when we are willing to listen to him. The chemicals open up, the gloves go back on, and the scrubbing begins. Pin sol all over the floors first with mops and scrub brooms. Bleach on the counters and butcher blocks. I follow what everybody else is doing and scrub hard and fast. Dick returns with a water hose and has Scotty open up one of the small port holes that lead to the outside of the ship.

"All hands out of the slaughterhouse when sprayin'. You're up, Greenhorn. Spray the area down and then use the squeegee to push it out through the ship's port hole. Scotty, stay with him make sure it's done right."

Scotty turns to me with a pair of safety glasses and a face mask. "Put these on. Don't start the hose 'til everyone clears out and do your best not to let any of those cleaners get in your eyes."

"I know… Some of that stuff was some pretty potent shit. I can feel my nose hairs burnin' off in my nostrils."

He laughs, "That's the spirit, Greenhorn. Have some fun with it." Everyone heads out in a hurry. "All right, kiddo. Spray her down!!" Then he runs out of the room too.

Bubbles and soap suds splash everywhere. At this rate, a shower will only be needed to get the smell of bleach off of me, but at least I'll be sanitized. The water hose does most of the work for me, but I squeegee the rest out through the port hole to drain out the side of the ship. Once the water hose is rolled up, I lift it over my shoulder to take it back up to the deck to be stowed away. The daylight has left us since we've down in the slaughterhouse. I can hear the guys smoking and joking as they try to get some form of food cooked in the kitchen. Then I realize that Yellow Jack never snuck in to prep a meal for us while we were cleaning things in the slaughterhouse. Not my place to ask, so I head up to the deck anyway to put away the water hose.

The ship has come to a crawl or a near stop in the choppy waters. Ever since the land went out of sight, I feel like I have been walking sideways or at a constant tilt in one direction or the other. The spotlight from the wheelhouse is on, but it's pointed to the side of a ship. Yellow Jack climbs up from the side but doesn't notice me in the darkness of the side of the deck I'm on. Another unfamiliar face follows him on board, but the skipper is coming down the steps with the bags I remember Yellow Jack bringing on board the first night I was on the ship. The bags appear heavy when the skipper hands them over, and the men that know Yellow Jack are all speaking Spanish quietly to each other. I can't hear what the skipper is saying to any of them. It's a speedboat next to the ship. An elaborate speedboat with a canvas style roof that the spotlight is shining on. How close are we to Newfoundland for a speed boat to make it out to us this far? Why is Yellow Jack getting offloaded here and not at port?

"What are you doing here?"

It's Dick, scowling at me from the entry that heads down below.

"How long you been standing there? Answer me now!"

"I was just putting the water hose away. We finished cleaning up everything in the slaughterhouse and…" shuddering under my breath from the cold and gripping the rails.

"I thought I told all you guys to get below, chow down and then bed down?" His voice grows more serious as he walks closer.

I look over to the skipper and all the men with Yellow Jack have smaller weapons or Uzis on them. Even Yellow Jack is making sure I see the pistol he is carrying. Skipper just holds his shaky hands up at them and shakes his head no. He looks like a nervous wreck too. I don't know what he said to them, but they stash their weapons back under their raincoats and load up on their speedboat as I hear the engine start up. The skipper keeps talking to them, as they throw a single bag up to him on the deck. He looks inside the bag and I see him glance at stacks of red and orange bills before closing the bag and giving them a thumbs up. But both of his hands are shaking.

"What the fuck is going on here, Dick?"

But that's when I notice the tire iron in his hand, and he has gotten a lot closer than I would like.

"You guys are runnin' drugs into Canada, aren't you?"

I grip the brass handle of the water hose on my opposite side of Dick, ready to swing it at him if he raises that tire iron at me.

"This isn't your concern, Greenhorn. Best you head back below and not remember anything you saw."

Before he says another word, he looks to see the speedboat taking off into the night. The engine's roar keeps his attention and I sling the brass hose end across his face to send him to the deck in pain.

"My name... Is Isaac, Dickhead!!"

I look and the skipper just saw what happened. I run down the steps to find the rest of the guys. All I have to do is follow the cigarette smoke all the way to the kitchen. I slam the kitchen door closed behind me, but there is no lock. Out of breath from too much smoking, I look out the small port hole of the door to see if they are following down yet. The crew just sits at the table, Iceman with a spoon up to his mouth, wondering why I'm so freaked out.

"Yellow Jack... He... He just got off loaded... Drugs... Guns..."

"Whoa... What's going on, kid? Yellow Jack always dead heads 'til we get close enough to Canada," Scotty says.

I start putting chairs against the door and checking out the port hole, but I must have knocked Dick out and the skipper is helping him.

"We don't have a lot of time. Guys, listen to me. I'm not lying to you. I don't have any reason to lie. Does the captain or the deck boss always make you stay below when they offload Yellow Jack?"

They all shake their head yes but remain confused.

"All the bags. All his luggage. It's all drugs or somethin' like that."

They look at me, totally stunned now.

Diesel speaks up, "I think you need to get some sleep there, Greenhorn. We were all just sayin' you been good out here with us these last few days and..."

I interrupt, "I know what I fucking saw! They offloaded several bags with Yellow Jack onto a speedboat and gave the skipper one bag back. Dick is up on deck right now with a cracked skull 'cause he was about to do the same to me just for seeing the drop happen. You get up to that wheelhouse and I'll bet you the skipper's got a bag of cash stashed away up there."

They all look at each other and think, trying to make sense of it all.

"Come on guys. Why would I lie about this?" Terrified, I continue to hold the door closed.

"The skipper never lets us in the wheelhouse for longer than a few minutes," Scotty says.

"We've never seen Yellow Jack get offloaded out at sea," Iceman adds in.

"And we never see what he brings with him on board since he started boarding with us a while ago," claims Diesel.

"They just made the trade, men with guns, and Yellow Jack went with them. Yellow Jack follows the drugs. And now they're making the run the rest of the way to Canada at night in a speedboat. I don't know what type of drugs or what they're smuggling or how much cash they gave the skipper. It was red cash, I think. Dick is in on this too, but I just slammed his face with the water hose…"

"Red?" asks Scotty.

"Yeah… It was, like… Red or orange looking cash… Or?"

"That's Canadian money," he says.

They all get up in a hurry before I have a chance to finish.

"Wait... Wait!?! What are we gonna do?"

Comanche doesn't hold back and bursts through my sad attempt at barricading the kitchen door. We all follow behind him. Once on deck, Diesel grabs the tire iron that Dick must have dropped. He and the skipper are up in the wheelhouse, not paying attention to what's happening on the deck. We all rush to the wheelhouse and my adrenaline makes me stumble up the stairs behind them. They all pile up at the door before Comanche kicks it in. The skipper just crouches down over his bag of money, looking up at Diesel with his tire iron at the ready.

"I been locked up over this drug shit before, Skip. I ain't goin' back to prison over somebody else's doin' this same shit again!" Diesel yells, as we all rush in.

The skipper looks completely overwhelmed and stands with his hands up. His hands are still shaking, and he's breathing fast and heavy. Eyes bloodshot. A small brick with white powder is open on the counter near maps and paperwork.

"Jesus, he's coked out of his mind," says Iceman.

"Hey Greenhorn..." one says from behind.

And Dick sends a blindsided punch at me as I stand in the doorway. His fist lands right on my lip and knocks me down to the steel walkway that leads into the wheelhouse. I shake the stars off as I get back on my feet. Every one of the crew is attempting to punch and push Dick out of the way to get to the skipper. I stand up and see him covering his stash of drugs and reaching under one of the control panels. I stumble upright just in time to see a pistol in the skipper's wobbly hand pointed at one of the guys as they wrestle around on the floor with Dick still. None of the crew knows that the skipper has the gun pointed at them.

"Wait!!! Wait!!!" I yell.

BANG!!!

He shoots a round off, and everyone goes silent. Iceman and Scotty hold their ears from the ringing. We all look at the skipper. He shot a round out one of the wheelhouse windows, which is now shattered but hasn't fallen in. I can taste the blood from my lip, but everyone first focuses on the cracked window, then turns to look at the skipper still pointing a gun at us.

"The next one *WILL* hit one of you."

Everyone slowly gets up and Dick pushes them all out of the way to get closer to the captain who keeps the gun pointed at us. All I keep looking at is the bullet hole in the window of the wheelhouse. Then I look to Comanche and see that he is beyond fuming. I don't think the skipper has enough bullets to stop him if he got any more pissed than he is right now.

"You've been a drug mule for cocaine over international waters into Canada?" asks Scotty, out of breath as he gets up on his feet. "Do they know you've been skimming them off the top from their supply? Jesus Walsh… What have you gotten us into?"

Skipper Walsh's hands just shake as he wipes his nose. His New England Patriot's hat raises just enough to see how crazed and bloodshot his eyes are. He lowers the gun, but he's too far away for any of us to make the jump on him. Especially with Dick right beside him.

"You knew about this too, Dick?" Scotty asks.

Diesels drops his tire iron on the floor in defeat. Iceman lowers the fillet knife I didn't even know he was carrying.

"I come for fish… No drugs," Comanche says in his brash and angered voice.

"How are you gonna turn all that hundreds and thousands of dollars into U.S. currency without raising suspicion? What's gonna happen when those people find out you shorted them of their stash, and they paid you for the whole thing?" I ask.

"I've gone this far unnoticed, you fuckin' pricks!!!" Skipper says, while waving the gun around frantically at us.

"We can do this the easy way or the hard way. The easy way gets you guys a lot more of the pot when this boat comes in meeting a full quota of fish and keeping your mouths shut," says Dick.

"And the hard way is getting ourselves shot all to hell over a bunch of coke we didn't even know you had on board 'til now, Skip. I didn't sign up for this! I met people like that in the slammer. They'll shoot you up just to watch you die before they sink the boat!" Diesel tells them both.

"They haven't noticed yet, and this is the last time!" Yells the skipper.

Scotty walks closer to him and he raises his gun back at his face. Scotty stops while staring down the barrel, "I've been with you a long time, Walsh. You're used up and fried out of your wits from that shit you've been snortin', mate. But we ain't mates no more… And they will come for you. They'll come for all of us, God Dammit!!!" He stomps his foot and curls his fists in a ball.

Skipper points the gun right at Scotty's temple and leans in close. "This life of fishing is at an end for us, old friend. Over fished waters, too small of quotas, child support for kids I don't see, alimony, paying for a house I don't even fuckin' live in. Paying you assholes. Cost of running this ship. This way of life is *shit* for all of us and I'm not ending it all with nothing to show for it! This was the biggest and the last haul for me. Consider all your pots larger than the last time."

He cocks the hammer back. "Now… Either you worthless lil' shits finish fishing for this damn trip's quota, and we all go home with more money than we ever had before thanks to me… Or else, I'll gut you all up like fish myself and turn you into bait for the net."

Chapter 9 - St. Elmo

The sea is now ravaging the ship with no mercy. Tensions are high. Returning to port is all any of us want to do, because it feels more like being held captive on this ship with nowhere to truly escape now. Hostages to the skipper's greed and any that may return looking for him. Dick even took the other guys' phones out of their belongings when we were bringing in a net earlier. Each catch at this point in our distressing journey, though small compared to when we first began, takes every ounce of time and energy through our exhaustion. The deck boss refuses to help us now. He stays close to the captain, and they both rotate in and out of the wheelhouse. Sleep is out of the question. Nobody has attempted to sleep since the fishing began. We are all uneasy and short with each other, even though we know that none of us is the true enemy here. Any conversation, especially in trying to deal with this mess, has to happen in whispers below the deck, out of earshot of the skipper and Dick.

"What's stopping either of them from killin' us and sending us overboard in the middle of the North Atlantic?" Iceman asks, as we clean fish in the slaughterhouse.

"Offing one of us and blame it on being lost at sea would be nothing new if anyone asked questions. But all four of us? He won't risk it. Not with that amount of cash on hand," I tell him.

Comanche cuts and cleans each fish with serious frustration. I turn to see Scotty more depressed and saddened by the situation.

"Maybe we can tell him to lay off the coke for the rest of the trip and we'll go along with it. There's no tellin' how many times he's done this before we found out. What harm could it really do if we just go along with it?" Diesel explains to us.

"He's drugged outta wit's end. He won't trust us, not with Dick whisperin' in his ear. You saw it Diesel. You too Comanche. I knew that last greenhorn losin' his hand wasn't no accident on his part. I think he saw somethin' like we just did, and Dick tried to make it look like an accident when he lifted that crane up just in time to slice off his hand. Nothin' else makes sense." Scotty looks up at me, "I wouldn't let a newbie get hurt that bad. A few bumps and cuts, sure, but not takin' off his entire hand. I think Dick tried to kill him lettin' that cable out the way he did."

Iceman collects all the fish scrap buckets and brings in his two cents, "Say we do get on their good side, then what? We return to port and trust the skipper to hand over our share of drug money after he switches the currency to American. You guys heard him. He's been at this for months and this is the last time. He's been prepping up for an extended vacation somewhere for months now. Dick probably doesn't even know what his end game is."

"All I'm sayin' is, maybe we let them think we're on their good side and as soon as their guard is down, we get the drop on them. Put a cap in both of them assholes," Diesels says.

"Then what are we gonna do with the money and the drugs still on board? That's just the money talkin' to you now," I tell him.

"Hey, fuck you, Greenhorn!" Diesel slaps a raw fish at me. Its guts hit my shoulder and splatter.

In a fit of anger, I push the entire table at him, making him lose balance with the already tossing ship. I jump over the slippery table ready to start swinging, but Comanche grabs my entire torso. "Fuck you Diesel! You think you're some hard ass because you've been locked up before and been sailing for a while? You're the same type of weasel that'll be the first to start bitchin' when you don't get your way in the Navy or it gets hard. You're a loser, just like the rest of us in all this. That's why the money matters to you so fuckin' much!"

Comanche turns me around, "Enough..." He just shakes his head at me and pushes me beside him. Diesel jumps up with a fury. Now Comanche and Iceman have to keep us apart. "Enough!" Comanche yells louder, while he spreads us apart with his massive reach and powerful grip. The back of my mind tells me that Diesel is not the problem here, but all I want to do is beat some sense into him.

The door to the slaughterhouse slams open. "What's going on down here with you bunch of girls?" Dick says.

"Nothin', asshole," Scotty says to him, as the rest of us get our bearing back.

Dick just stares at us from the doorway for a bit. "We need all hands on deck. Skipper wants a word with all of you."

"We'll clean off and be up in a sec," Scotty tells him.

Dick slams the door shut and makes his way back up. Scotty turns to us, "You two wankers quit your bickering. None of us down here are the problem. And *you* should know better, Navy boy. Now, make amends..." Diesel and I stare back at each other in stubbornness. "Now," says Scotty more firmly. I finally reach out to shake and Diesel does the same. We clean up and find that the skies have darkened since we've been down below, and the seas have calmed down. It's odd though. Lightning and thunder can be heard in the distance, yet the seas are black and quiet. Not a ripple to be heard splashing against the side of the ship. Only our shivering breaths from the cold can be seen beyond the spotlight that lights up the deck. The lightning is far off, but the thunder feels closer.

The skipper, standing next to Dick at the wheelhouse doorway, motions us to come up the stairs. His pistol stays tucked in his belt on the right side of his waist. When he motions his hands, they don't seem as shaky. But I can't get a good glimpse of his eyes with the spotlight near him to see if they are still red from a recent line snort of cocaine like he was earlier.

"Well folks…" The skipper lights up a cigar, "We just got word there's a major storm between us and any port southeast of us. I want the freezers locked down, and the nets stowed away. Everything on deck needs to be locked down. We hit over eighty percent of our quota, and that's good enough for me. We can't risk bringin' in any more fish, and we can't risk opening and closing the freezers for extended periods."

He could never speak that fluently if he was drugged out of his mind again, but we all saw the stash he had somewhere in that wheelhouse. Not to mention the loads of cash.

"Are we gonna push through the storm to head back, Skip?" Diesel asks.

He takes another puff of his cigarette, "No… We're gonna wait it out a few days and steam in. That slight warm front is stirring up a lot of shit. That's where all that lightning is coming from. Hurricane force winds are coming right behind that."

"But what about those drug smugglers? We're sitting ducks out here if they come back," Diesels pleads again.

"If they feel the need to brave a storm in a tiny speedboat, then they'll never make it back to us. We sit and we wait…" Skipper Walsh pulls out his pistol, but it stays pointed towards the ground. "Is that understood?!?!"

Comanche and Scotty turn their backs and start to walk down the steps to the deck. Iceman and I refuse to answer the skipper's demands, so we ignore him and join Scotty and Comanche. Diesel just seems more concerned than any of us and doesn't know which way to go, continue pleading with the captain to return home or walk away to stow away the nets with the rest of us.

"I SAID!!!… Is that understood, you bunch of pricks!?!?!" Skipper yells at the top of his lungs.

Scotty turns around in a fury, "The only thang understood here is you're too much a coward to face anything that puts your recent loot in harm's way, but you'll gladly put your crew in harm's way! And that's no skipper of mine, aye Walsh!?!?"

"You wanna have a fuckin' go with me, old man!?!?" Skipper shouts, as he waves his pistol around at all of us.

"Yeah, I'll have a go!! I'll have a go with you, you lying bastard!!"

I tap Comanche on the shoulder to grab Scotty before this conversation gets any worse. The biggest and the most aggressive man on the ship, with little English in his vocabulary, is the one to count on not to start a fight or let any others do the same. He grabs Scotty and lifts him off his feet. Scotty keeps damning the skipper and flailing around.

"You'll get us all killed, or in jail one. I fuckin' dare them to put me in a jail cell with you. You fucking wanker!!" Scotty yells back the same things over and over, but the skipper just stays up on those steps with his pistol in hand, ready for anything. The lightning all around us in the distance becomes like a multitude of strobe lights. And now, the thunder moves closer to us.

We get Scotty calmed down and Dick keeps the spotlight on us while we move down to the deck. I can hear a buzzing static. Nothing like I ever heard before.

"Scotty…" I try to interrupt him, but he keeps cursing the skipper. "Scotty, shut up!!!" I tell him. He finally shuts up, surprised I was willing to yell at him over anything. "Do you guys hear that?"

"Hear what?" Iceman asks.

"Sounds like static, I think. Like a radio buzzing, or something."

Everyone is silent and looking around. The static sound grows more intense and louder. I look up at the skipper and Dick, but they are just as confused. Especially when they see the same blue glow that the rest of us see behind them. Every antenna and pole sticking up from the wheelhouse, even parts of the crane winch cables, all have the same blue glow growing from them. Each second that passes, it becomes brighter and the sound of static turns into an electric buzz. We all watch and wait in a tense silence.

"What the hell is that?" Iceman asks, loud enough to be heard over the electrical buzz that radiates from the antennas.

Nobody says anything. Nobody knows what to say. Any and all high points on the ship have the same blue glow. Glowing so hot is seems to be turning purple.

A flash bright enough to blind slams down on the ship's wheelhouse and sends us all to the deck for cover.

"Holy shit!?!?" I yell with my face down.

Someone else shouts, "Lightning!!!"

Sparks fly everywhere from the wheelhouse. The lights go out and we are in complete darkness. That's when it hits. A booming sound of the following thunder hits so hard the gear on the deck rumbles off the floor and falls over.

The thunder rumbles on, looming all around us and underneath us it feels. The entire ship has been blacked out of power. The lightning strike has fried something, but everyone is either too afraid or too stunned to talk right now. Just panting and heavy breathing from all of us still crouching down if another lightning strike hits.

Someone gets up to their feet and shuffles around blindly. "All hands... All hands... Sound off mates!" That's Scotty talkin' to us in the dark.

"I'm good," I tell him. He's close enough to me that I can see his shape.

"I'm up," Iceman says.

"All good," Diesel grumbles.

"Good..." Comanche says with his deep voice in the pitch black.

"Diesel, you get down below and power up the backup generators ASAP," yells Dick, still up the stairs of the wheelhouse.

"I'm on it," Diesel replies. He uses a lighter to light his way.

"Are we up, Scotty!?! Is anybody hurt?!" Skipper asks.

Scotty answers him and I make my way to my feet. The ship's antennas are glowing red hot still. Some sparks are still coming from the wheelhouse, but I see the skipper moving around inside to get it under control before a fire breaks out. The sparks are clouded out with a fire extinguisher that I can hear being sprayed.

I use Diesel's method of lighting my way with my lighter, but it must have gotten moisture inside of it while laying down on the deck's wet surface. I struggle with it in total blackness. The only light I can get at the moment is the lightning strikes in the distance that brighten the deck for a few milliseconds. My hands are too cold and numb to keep trying to light it. I blow on the top to get any moisture out, but I hear breathing close by in the blackness. Maybe not breathing. More like hissing or whispering.

"Scotty, is that you?" I motion my hands out, still blinded in the darkness. My hand touches something. But it isn't the raincoat material of anyone on this ship. Another lightning strike in the distance lights up the shape of a person in front of me dressed in black, still whispering something I can't understand. More lightning from the distance. A fluttering black cloth or dress moves with the slight breeze felt. I turn around to see Scotty helping the skipper and Dick in the wheelhouse.

I look down to flick my lighter to see what's in front of me. It finally lights up in front of me. It's the same woman I saw on the first night, and I am motionless in shock and dread. She turns around, head looking down, with dark hair covering her face. Until she lifts her head and looks at me with those black eyes. Eyes that have no soul or emotion. Dead eyes. Her hands, shaky and feeble, reach out to me as her head tilts.

I start to back away in panic, but she moves slowly and decrepit like. A withering step forward to me as she keeps whispering. Her head tilts more in her feeble walk towards me in the dark, with my tiny lighter showing more of her white face. A face that is not white, just frozen white and missing skin in places down to the bone beneath it. The only color I see on her is red. The red blood endlessly flows from her cut open throat.

She comes closer, but I stumble on something on the deck and drop my lighter. Too scared and frozen in fear to get up and scream for help. I still see her shape, but the only light I have is the lightning moving further and further away. My hands scramble to look for my lighter on the deck, but I can't find it. She hovers over me, but her feet don't touch the ground.

Looking down at me, she whispers the same thing, over and over, "May you burn in the bay… Burn in the bay."

I kick my feet to crawl away from her while still on the hard deck. Something drops and thuds down on the deck right in front of me. I find my lighter again. I must have created a gushing blister on my thumb trying to get it lit and I see her still standing in front of me. But her head is at my feet on its side, still gushing blood from her hollow throat.

She whispers again and again.

She doesn't stop saying the same thing.

"Burn in the bay…"

Chapter 10 - Shrapnel

"Get these fucking lights on!!!" I yell. I can't believe what I'm seeing. My lighter goes out and I can't take it anymore.

"We're working on it," someone yells back.

I scramble to my feet and rush back closer to the wheelhouse. Taking cover from the lightning strike must have sent me further away from everyone else. I walk quickly, but still blindly, just to get away from her. "There's someone here. There's something on the ship, dammit!"

"What are you talking about?" Iceman says. I think it's Iceman. It sounds like him.

The lights finally turn back on and the spotlight shines in the same direction I just stumbled from. There's nothing there. I run into Comanche, still getting on his feet too.

"Comanche. Did you see that? I'm not crazy. Tell me you saw that?" I shake his arm like a madman.

He just looks at me, more concerned than confused. I point where the spotlight shines and neither of us sees anything. Just the deck and a few items scattered around that weren't secured to something. He just keeps looking back at me, puzzled and worried now. He walks further down the deck where I keep pointing but sees nothing. He walks back to me into the light and shakes his head no. Not a *no* in confusion, but a *no* in concern for what I just saw to make me so startled.

"I got it Skip..." Diesel comes back up from below. "We've blown a few breakers and we're running on battery power right now. We got enough juice to crank the engine, but not long after that."

"Help him get the engines started, Scotty. We're adrift right now. We gotta have the engines charging up the power batteries to see what that lightning fried up on us."

"On it," says Scotty.

It looks like Dick is behind the spotlight. He points it up above the wheelhouse and spots the damage of the antennas and gear above. Wiring, with sparks flickering from them, just flap around in the breeze.

"Iceman!!" Dick yells out. "Get up there and assess the damage for us. We need that antenna back up to get our radio going." Iceman commits to getting up the rest of the stairs to the wheelhouse.

I turn to Comanche, still stowing away gear. "Comanche…" He turns to look at me. "There's something on this boat." He just pauses. I don't know if he believes me from the look on my face or if he doesn't have the words to respond at all in English. He just stares, still bothered by what I am saying.

The engines crank back up after several attempts. The lights go brighter, and I can see everyone, including Iceman investigating the damage on the antennas above the wheelhouse.

"It's pretty bad up here, Skip," Iceman yells down to the wheelhouse. "We gotta replace a lot of fried wiring and get a spare antenna put in place if we got one."

The skipper just shakes his head and curses under his breath. Dick is still scrambling around in the wheelhouse, with Scotty at the engine controls.

"Wouldn't be much use. That damn lightning surge fried the radio up too. Even if we got a new antenna put up, it wouldn't fix that mess. Get down from there, Iceman," Scotty tells him.

"That's alright, man. Lightning never hits the same spot twice. Right? We're damn lucky on that one, 'cause all we lost was the radios," Iceman says in sarcasm that nobody finds humorous at the moment.

I hear another boom in the distance. A thunderous boom that doesn't sound like normal thunder. But there wasn't a flash of lightning to go with it. Where's the lightning?

"Oh my God… Iceman, get down off there!!! Everybody, get down!!!" I yell at the top of my lungs.

An explosive crash goes blasting through the wheelhouse as Iceman tries to jump down. Glass and shrapnel are shattered everywhere on the deck on top of me and Comanche as we drop. He lands on top of me and his bulk takes the winds out of my lungs. His backside takes the grunt of the wood and metal that bounces around like weightless ashes.

"That's fuckin' cannon fire," someone yells.

"Help!!!... Help me!!!"

That's Iceman screaming. He's landed on the deck and I get up from under Comanche's weight to help Iceman. His torso has a multitude of glass and metal shards piercing him. I run to him and blood pours from his mouth as he screams in agony.

"What the hell was that explosion?" yells Diesel, while coming back up from the engine room again. "What the…" He stops and sees me running to Iceman, blood filling up the deck space all around him as he gurgles for air.

I drop down next to him to look him over. "Get him to the wheelhouse now!!! Move the ship before they fire again! Help me get him up, Comanche!!"

Without hesitation, Scotty revs up the motors, and the ship moves out of the line of fire it was in. Comanche and I carry him up the stairs. Once we're in the wheelhouse, Skipper and Dick look stunned and lost on what to do. Iceman just struggles and chokes on his blood while flinching around. Diesel brings over the first aid kit. Scotty is behind the wheel and still getting the boat to start moving away, while looking over his shoulder to see what's going on. I look through the kit and cut his jacket and shirt open with a random fillet knife.

"Call for a chopper to get him outta here!" I tell the skipper.

"Radio's fried," he says in a lowly scared voice.

My hands are covered in blood. Once his shirt is off, I can see that metal and glass shrapnel is through his lung. One piece of railing punctured vertically through his thigh and out over his shoulder. The screaming, along with painful moaning, stops and he starts shaking violently. I keep pressure on his wounds, but there are just too many cuts. Blood is everywhere on me.

"Stay with us Iceman! Diesel, lift his legs. He's going into shock. Comanche, just take his hand and talk to him. Keep him awake while I try to…"

Nobody moves. I look around at all their faces and see defeat. Iceman has stopped shaking and his eyes stay wide open. I reach up to feel for a pulse, but there is nothing. He's lost too much blood, too many lacerations. I can't even attempt CPR on him without hurting him more with that rail lodged in his torso. Comanche holds his hand for a bit longer, but it's no use. Iceman has died from what I think was a cannon blast. Comanche lets his hand go, and it drops to the floor, limp.

We all look around at each other in silence. Scotty keeps looking over his shoulder, but I can tell he's getting emotional watching one of the youngest crewmates go out violently like that. Everyone is silent, but I look right at the skipper, who is now holding his pistol out at his side. His hands are shaking again from the withdrawals of his new drug habit or maybe he's just as scared as the rest of us.

The radio brings in static. A loud static that jolts all of us out of our trance from watching Iceman die.

"That's not possible," Dick says.

"It's just wires frying up and going through the speakers," says the skipper.

The static comes in and out. I reach down to close Iceman's eyes. We wait and listen, hoping for a miracle that a voice would come through.

Diesel steps over me and Iceman and reaches for the mic on the radio, "Hello?! Is anybody there?!?! Hello? Is anybody there?! They gonna kill us out here. We need help…"

Nobody answers Diesel's frantic pleas for help. Nobody can answer. Some pieces of the leftover antenna may be in our friend's stomach from the blast. Diesel doesn't even notice until Scotty points out that the main power cord for the radio is fried up from the lightning strike. Diesel just lowers his head in defeat. I take my coat off and cover Iceman. I've never seen a dead body while working in the med bays of the aircraft carriers in the Navy. You grow numb to a lot of gore as a medic, but I'll never get used to seeing a dead body. This was my first one, and it was an unnecessary death.

"They're coming for us, aren't they? The drug runners," Scotty asks.

Nobody answers. Even the skipper looks down, but keeps a death grip on that pistol.

The static from the radio keeps going in and out. Diesel just desperately holds the mic, listening in. The static goes out again for a longer pause, then the white noise changes. A screeching sound so harsh you'd want to rip your ears out. Several tones come in and out, but it is overall just scratchy music notes. We all just listen intently as to what may be coming over the radio, but the goosebumps raise on the back of my neck because I know it isn't human. The whispers I heard from the thing I saw on deck come through the mic in a jumbled mess, mixed with other tones. I recognize those whispers, but nobody else does. They are more focused on the noise coming through, but those are becoming recognizable too.

"Is that whales?" Diesels asks, with the mic still pressed against his ear.

"Whales don't sound like that," Scotty answers.

"No… That's a very out-of-tune violin coming through the radio," I tell them.

Everyone seems more frightened now than ever. Of all the things that's happened since coming up from below deck, those creepy noises coming through a broken radio puts the fear of God in us all. The white noises, the violin tunes, the whispers, and the static grow louder to the point that Diesel just slams the mic down on the table. We all look at the radio and just listen in horror.

Comanche stands up and approaches the skipper. He goes to raise his pistol at him, but Comanche holds his hand with the pistol down while he puts his other hand at the skipper's throat and lifts him up. In his deep voice and his hand gripped around the skipper's throat he tells him, "You kill us all…"

Comanche slowly lets the skipper's throat go and he catches his breath.

Then all goes quiet from the radio while we watch Comanche step away.

Not even the static is coming through, but we all hear a struggled breathing.

Now, only white noise and breathing is clear until a dark raspy voice is heard saying,

"I... Die..."

Chapter 11 - The Sea Whispers

We all sat and listened to the radio in the wheelhouse until the morning hours. Nothing ever came back through the speakers though. Looking all around us into the sea, there are no signs of life that could hear the air horns on the ship. Nothing in the sky that could see distress flares. There's just nothing out here but a deafening silence and a terror filling our nerves. Something is after us, and it has enough firepower to send this ship into a watery grave.

The skipper and Dick send us away as they try to repair the radio. Scotty and Diesel wrap Iceman up after a mild cleaning of his wounds. No one thinks to bring body bags on a commercial fishing charter. So, they use an emergency space blanket style sleeping bag to keep him covered. Enough tape makes his remains airtight inside the bag. They plan to leave his remains in an empty space in the freezer until we return to port. If we ever return at this point.

I grabbed the first aid kit from the wheelhouse on my way out to work on Comanche's backside and remove some of the shrapnel. I have to cut most of his shirt off. His torso is covered in more tribal tattoos than his face is, but I can see several previous scars he had before the glass and wood imbedded in him.

"Some of this older scar tissue may have saved your ass there, Comanche."

He says nothing in return as I pull out some glass pieces with tweezers. Not a flinch from him with each piece of debris that comes out. He's just angrier and more tense since we came back down below. When the needle for stitching goes in, I don't even think to warn him. If he hasn't flinched or shown any level of pain by now, he either has a high pain tolerance or just doesn't show pain, or both. After more cleaning, I cover all the cuts, with or without stitches, with a bandage to keep them covered. My gloves come off and I move over to face him.

"Try to keep these bandages on and keep the wounds as clean as you can. All of them were clean cuts, but there's always a chance of infection. If you need help changing any of them, just let me know, alright?"

He shakes his head yes and stands up from his seat, towering over me again. I hold up my hand to stop him before he walks away. He seems confused, but I need to say this, "I can't thank you enough for what you did. I think if I was still facing the wheelhouse before we all hit the deck, everything that is lodged in your back may have ended up in my face and we'd be piecing together my cheeks off the floors. So… I thank you." I place my arm on his shoulder. He does the same to my shoulder and shakes his head.

Diesel and Scotty come out from the freezer, but they are definitely not the same. Down on themselves, for obvious reasons. I may be out of my depth here, but I feel I have to say something. They all sit down near the slaughter table and light up their smokes. Comanche walks over to the door to see if anyone is listening in.

"Guys, I know I'm still the new guy here, but I am sorry about all this. All you guys have been working together for a while… I was really trying to…"

Scotty just holds up a hand to silence me. "You did more than most there, matey."

"We know you were tryin'," Diesel adds in. "Didn't none of us know what to do after that and seein' him all busted up like that bleedin' all over the place. But you tried."

Comanche stays by the door keeping an eye out for Dick and the skipper. He gives us all the thumbs up.

Diesel opens up first, "We need to get help out here, Scotty. Them drug runners are gonna come out here lookin' for their money and drugs Skip took from them. And I heard their warning loud and clear."

"One guy is already dead over this. Why won't the skipper just head into the nearest port on the Canadian side?" I ask.

Scotty takes a puff of his smoke, trying to think. "We can't risk takin' on a storm like what brought on that lightning. I've seen that before and it'll get ugly. Cold fronts, warm fronts, heavy currents and winds. Whatever storm the skipper was talkin' 'bout before the lightning hit, it's gonna be big. Going through that without proper navigation or radio if things go to shit? Hell, nobody even knows our current location, much less if we get broadsided by a wave. I know Walsh. I been with him for a while. Comanche will say the same thing. He won't risk it. With or without however much money he has onboard."

I look over at Comanche and he shakes his head yes, agreeing with Scotty.

"Can that radio be fixed?" Diesel asks.

"They're up there trying, but that lightning strike fried everything up. You were lucky to get the engines goin' again, but all those systems are separate. We try and push through that storm, then we go in blind with ol' school nav tricks, mates. And my skipperin' days have passed ways back."

"So… What do we do?" I ask.

"We get that fuckin' gun away from them two assholes and make a run for it after we throw them overboard," Diesel says with more sarcasm and attitude.

I keep my mouth shut this time so not to mention the fact that his plan involves taking the drugs and the money for ourselves, if the skipper and Dick are just tossed over. At this point, I want no part of that drug money. Not at the expense of more people getting killed over it.

"No… Right now, we wait for the storm to die off. Could be a few days, but we just gotta wait. Think of how to handle this in the meantime," Scotty says while holding his head in his hands. He sighs and lifts his head up. "We just gotta wait…"

"That's some bullshit. Them drug runners know we're fuckin' here, Scotty. We throw Dick over first and then the skipper will have no one watchin' his back," Diesel says frantically, not realizing his voice raising in his growing panic.

"We're not gonna do that," Scotty replies.

"Oh yeah. Makin' sure you, and you, and you, and me," as he points at each of us, "eats a fuckin' bullet and wakes up dead, just means that there's one less person who can rat him out. OR!?! One less person he has to split his drug money with. And splittin' the haul for this damn catch of fish ain't nothin' compared to what he just hauled in as a drug mule."

We all look at each other quietly. Everyone knows what the other is thinking. Everyone knows Diesel is absolutely correct. The only person that the skipper has on his side is Dick.

"Even if we do take the ship, how do we convince the coast guard that we weren't a part of this? Especially when there's a dead guy in the freezer," I ask.

"We're not taking the ship," Scotty says, lowering his head again. "We all smell like rotten' fish and lackin' sleep. I know we haven't ate a decent plate of grub in days since Yellow Jack left. Nobody's thinking straight in the head right now. We need to get some sleep, lads. Get a shower too, but one of us stays up at a time, just to be safe. Aye, mates?"

We all agree and get up to make our way out of the slaughterhouse. But I'm not gonna keep my mouth shut about what I saw this time. I might look crazy, but it's still fresh in my mind and I have to know what I saw. Comanche didn't blow off my claims of earlier. He seemed more concerned about it and if I see the same look on the rest of their faces when I mention it, then I'll know for certain that my lack of sleep hasn't gotten the best of me yet.

"There's something else, guys…"

They all stop, and I see Comanche has stepped in closer to the doorway. He looks at me and just motions to tell them the same thing I tried to tell him before

Iceman was killed on the deck. I take a deep breath, not knowing how this conversation is gonna go.

"There's something on this ship..." They all look at me confused, but I still have their attention. "I don't know what it is, and I've seen it twice now. The first time I thought I was just seeing things or lacking sleep. Then I saw it again."

"It?" Diesel asks.

"Yeah... Like, I can't explain it other than a woman on the ship, dressed in black. Dark hair. She kept her back to me the first time I saw her, but when the lightning hit and the lights went out, she turned around and looked at me."

"You go from an *it* to a woman on the ship. Which is it?" Scotty asks, showing more concern.

"I don't know... I thought it was nothing. Then I thought it was a woman. Now, I know it's something else. Something that's already dead and she is always whispering. Saying the same things over and over."

Comanche just looks at me, holding his palms out, and asks "What was said?"

"What makes you think this lady is already dead? How do you know it's a damn ghost or some shit, or someone snuck on board?" Diesel starts getting pissy again.

"Because her damn head fell off, and she kept saying the same thing over and over. Not to mention she was not walking towards me. She was more like, hovering over the deck."

Diesel just throws his hands up in the air as he sits back down, "Great. That's just great. Drug smugglers. A skipper that's got us hostage and coked out of his mind... Now, we got some evil spirits on board... Great! Just kill me now, 'cause brothers never make it outta shit like this."

"Shut up Diesel, you whiney lil' shit," Scotty scolds him and then turns back to me. "What was she sayin' there, lad?"

"*Burn in the bay*. She kept whispering it over and over. *Burn in the bay* over and over and I have no idea what that means."

Scotty just shakes his head and looks down.

"Whispering widow," Comanche says.

Just in hearing how he said that, I can tell that his level of concern is turning to fear. I'd like to think there isn't much that could scare somebody like him.

"What's he talkin' about, Scotty?" I ask.

"It's just a myth. Just old sea stories is all."

"That's right... It's just old sea tales from drunken sailors abroad," says Skipper Walsh from behind us.

We all get up in a hurry. Comanche wasn't watching the door when the skipper came in and we didn't notice him. He walks in closer with that pistol still at his side. His hands are shaky and his eyes bloodshot again.

He walks close enough to take a better look at all of us in our disturbed state. "I'll hear no talks of voodoo nonsense," he tells Comanche. "Nor old sea tales of cursed ships on my boat." He tells Scotty as he walks closer to him, "Iceman's death was a freak accident and nothing more. We all knew the risks coming out here."

"Cannon fire from your newest set of friends that you stole from is no accident," Scotty says, as they have an intense stare down.

He lifts the gun up to hold it at Scotty's torso. "If you don't like the way I skipper the boat, why don't you do better then, Scotty?"

Scotty just glares back at him. Trying to hold his tongue, "You keep pointing that gun at everybody, eventually you'll have to shoot somebody."

Trying to break the tension, I take a good look at the skipper, but I hear him breathing heavily and rapidly. "Are you fucking high again?"

The skipper turns to look at me now. Of all the things I could have said to break the tension in the room, and that's what comes out of my mouth. He walks closer to me and stuffs his pistol back into his waist belt. His head is shaky and sweaty too. He walks over back to the doorway and pulls out a cigar to light while leaning against the wall. "While you 'lil girls were down here planning my demise, did Dick come down here?"

"We thought he was up in the wheelhouse with you getting things fixed?" Diesel asks.

"We got the windows for the wheelhouse boarded up a while ago, but the radio's toast," he says. "So, Dick hasn't come down here at all?"

We all look at each other and shake our heads no.

"Maybe another freak accident up there Skip," I tell him with sarcasm.

He takes another puff of his cigar and blows out enough smoke to fill the already musty room. "Keep talkin' to me like that and it won't be the last freak accident there, Greenhorn." He turns to walk out. "Search the ship. Every room, every closet, and every bunk. Scour every inch of this ship and find him, assholes," he says, as he walks back up to the deck.

Diesel and Comanche split paths out of the slaughterhouse to go looking in the other rooms and the engine bay area. Scotty looks around in the freezer area, but I grab his attention at the doorway before he walks out.

I grab him by the arm and motion to stay quiet. "What is going on out there? Do you guys know what I saw, 'cause Comanche sure acts like he does?"

He looks around outside the doorway to make sure we're alone. "The whispering widow is not the problem. She's a victim, but it's just an old seaman's tale, or more like a warning of sorts. The real problem is what happens after you see her. It's a pirate ship that comes and destroys everything in its path... A ship with sails that never stop burning."

There is no nice way of saying this to him, but I think he already knows that I am thinking everything he just said is absolute garbage. None of us are up for old sea stories right now with the problems we're dealing with.

"Don't believe me, do you?"

I just shake my head no, confused as to why Scotty would indulge in childish horror stories while hostage on a commercial fishing boat.

"Let me ask you, Isaac. How did you know it was cannon fire that was comin' in and took out my mate, Iceman, in that freezer dead now?"

"It just sounded familiar. You hear them go off when shooting cannons at Navy ceremonies and stuff like that. Veterans' burials have the salute with the cannons, and it just sounded the same."

"Drug mules in the North Atlantic waters wouldn't be shooting a single cannon at a lowly fishing vessel and risk sinking their own drugs and money. What kinda drug mule keeps a cannon at the ready?"

I can only imagine the look on my face, but what he says makes sense.

"Like I said when this all first started. Out here, we are all we got. Out here, the impossible can become possible. Without trust, that big blue ocean will swallow us up. And the lightning storm like we just seen a while ago, she's gettin' hungry there, young lad."

A knock at the door and I turn to open it. Comanche stands there with that same look of concern since I mentioned the whispering widow. "Come," is all he says and points to the deck.

Scotty and I head up with him and Diesel just looks out beyond the ship with a pair of binoculars.

"Did you two already search the ship?" Scotty asks.

"Yep… And he's hiding good enough somewhere to never be found, or he took a swim. I already told Skip and he ain't happy about it either. But his problems just got a lot bigger if he jumped ship while we were down below. Take a look at this."

He hands Scotty the binoculars so he can see too. The morning hours should have more daylight for us to work with by now. The overcast gets darker the further southwest we try to see with the binoculars. So dark, it would be easy to assume that it is still nighttime in the distance. Until you see a tiny bolt of lightning hitting the water's surface and hear a faint thunder in the distance. Just as the skipper said, a major storm system is between us and land while we have no navigation or radio.

I look behind me at the wheelhouse and see the skipper stands on the top of the stairs above all of us looking at the storm in the distance too. He puffs his cigar with a look of contempt for his bothered crew against him and now the storm. His only crew member on his side is now missing, but he still has that pistol ready to aim at whoever he pleases.

We all just stand on the deck looking at the approaching storm and wishing the waters would remain as calm as they are now, but we all know that may be unlikely. All the engines can do now is hold position against the current while we wait it out.

"Have you ever seen one that mean lookin', Scotsman?" Diesel asks.

"A few times, but never that dark this time of day."

"No good…" Comanche says, as he hands me the binoculars.

I look through and see a darkness that can only be described as a biblical evil. The thunder that roles in the distance with each lightning strike appears to be more like tiny neon threads. Thus, reminding me again of something else Scotty told me when this all began.

This is her world, not ours. We're just here fishin' in it. And she's reminding us of that as she whispers to us. More than just a whisper, though. It is a dark grumbling growl of vile thunder.

Chapter 12 - Blood Money

The skipper has barricaded himself into the wheelhouse. The only reason we know he's still functioning is the engines will start up occasionally to maneuver the boat against the currents and to stay away from the approaching storm as we wait it out. It's been a full day since Iceman was killed and the crew remains silent with petty things to keep us busy. Many of us sit and wonder what the actual plan is that the skipper has in mind for when the storm fades and we return to port. Will he split his drug money after washing it with U.S. currency somehow? How will he explain Iceman's death? How long has he been doing this? Are we all accessories to his crimes now? So many questions loom in our minds. But the paranoia we all have becomes more clear the less each of us speaks to the other about what has happened.

My own fears are that some may be turning to side with the skipper, knowing how much drug money he may have successfully brought in already. Dick had already sided with the skipper, but he has now been missing for an entire day. We searched the ship for a while longer for him. Until nobody could generate a full count of emergency life rafts. There's never been a need to count how many were available to the crew. It's just one of those things that you know you have somewhere on board, but never think to count how many you have. We leave Dick's demise up to braving a long paddle to the coast to save his own skin on a blow-up raft. Most of us couldn't care less, though. My lack of concern for our missing deck boss comes from knowing now that he may have had something to do with what happened to the last greenhorn. However, the crew's lack of concern for him missing may be that the less there are of a crew when, and if, we return, the bigger their pot of gold becomes. I don't know if I can trust anybody at this point. I have no doubt that everyone else feels the same way.

The typical chit-chat of their endeavors back home is non-existent. Sometimes we pass the time with some rounds of cards. But nothing can keep our minds off how the ship keeps rocking around in the choppy waters from the looming storm that slowly closes the distance on us. Scotty and Diesel mange to sleep some, but I'm sure it's with one eye open. None of us have had a decent meal since Yellow Jack was offloaded, which seems like forever ago now. Snack cakes, cheap coffee, chips, and cigarettes, for the most part, is our diet. Nobody trusts anybody to cook for the other now. It only took one day for us to get to this level of suspicion towards one another. I don't want to know what three or four more days of this waiting around will do to us.

I walk away from my lonely fifth hand of solitaire at the kitchen table and reach for my violin case under my bunk. Diesel just looks at me in contempt and rolls over in his bunk, saying nothing. I gear up and put on my beanie before heading up to the deck. I can't even see the skipper in the wheelhouse. Half of the windows are now boarded up from the cannon blast. He only has enough visibility to steer the ship, but not see anything happening on the deck. Not that we're still hauling anything in anyway.

The deck area is cold, gusty, and quiet. The boat feels as if it rocks around harder when walking around on the deck, but a good stable platform to sit down on makes all the difference when playing a violin in restless seas. I pull out the violin and stroke a few tunes. I always told myself, when I get out of the Navy, I'll be practicing everyday like I used to when I was still in high school. I always told my mother before I lost her that her paid lessons would never go to waste. I can't recall ever playing in front of my dad though. As far as playing in front of my ex-fiancé, well, I came up here to play, hoping to remind myself of better days. So, why bother thinking about that train wreck? The storms on the horizon instinctively create a somber tune to play alone here on the deck. I close my eyes to think of some better upbeat tunes, but that barely comes in after a few scratches of the bow. It gets harder to focus whenever I close my eyes and Iceman's terrified and bloody face springs into my thoughts.

It's no use, really. I can't think about anything other than everything that has already gone wrong, and I don't care to ruin this one thing either. Maybe I'll try again on a different day. I take the violin off my shoulder and move to put it away, but the storm in the distance holds my attention for a moment.

"Sad music…"

My heart skips a beat as I jump, startled at first until I realize it's Comanche sitting near a railing. I can see a slight grin on his face from scaring me. He stays wrapped in a blanket to keep warm, while smoking his pipe.

"Jesus Comanche… How does somebody as big as you go sneaking around so much?" I ask, while closing up the violin case and tuck it under my arm.

"No music?" Comanche asks, confused, as I walk over and sit with him.

"No… Not today, Comanche. I just can't stay focused enough to get into it right now, I guess. Maybe when things are better, you can hear me play it at my mom's old pub back home, yeah?"

He reaches his pipe over, "Smoke…"

"Oh no. Not this time, big guy… That stuff had me spinning for hours last time. I don't know how you smoke so much of it and still walk straight."

He grins again and goes back to puffing on his long pipe. We both stare at the storm for a while in the quiet, and I swear those clouds seem to get darker somehow.

"Care to tell me what the hell's going on out here, Comanche? You don't seem the type to scare easily. But when Scotty does the same after I mention what I saw, something tells me you guys know something I don't."

He just looks at me, straight faced. Maybe that was too much for his broken English to understand. He pulls his pipe away from his face and points at the inside of my collar. I look down and he's pointing at my necklace that came out and slightly hangs outside my shirt unknowingly.

"Oh… That's my St. Peter. My mom gave it to me before I left for the Navy."

He holds out his palm. I guess he wants to see it. I take it off from around my neck so he can get a closer look at it while he still smokes his pipe. He looks at it closely, but there's barely enough light left for him to see.

"It's a St. Peter. Where I'm from, they call him the patron of fishing. They hold him in very high regards there in the Catholic Church too. Peter and Paul were apostles of Christ, but Peter was a fisherman before that. Maybe after too, I think. But that's where the verse "make you fishers of men" came from when they went with Jesus."

He shakes his head yes as he hands it back to me, "The Christian God?" He asks.

"Yeah, well, sort of. I haven't been to mass in years. So, some of it has left my memory. Do they have churches where you're from?" Nothing from him. He just looks at me, still straight faced. "Do you ever say more than one or two words at a time? I know you know more English than you let on, Comanche."

He hands me the pipe again. I try to refuse, but he keeps pushing it towards my mouth. "Smoke more… Talk less," he says.

I hold a finger up. "Only if you tell me what you think is really going on out here. Deal?"

He shakes his head yes and I commit to taking a light smoke with him. The onslaught of coughing comes, and with an empty stomach, the buzz comes right away this time.

"My people talk of Sedna. She give life in all the waters," he pauses to take a smoke and passes it back to me. "She also give man the dead blue sea." He points to the storm, "That storm is dead blue sea out there. But when she give man fishing… Fishing is life."

I take another puff and hand it over to him. "The lady in black I saw on the deck. Is that this Sedna you're talking about? Like some sort of ghost?"

He shakes his head no. "The whispering widow is more death that brings death. Whispering widow is forever lost to the dead blue sea. Sedna give man two things through the sea. Life and death."

"Sedna, yeah?"

He shakes his head yes, but pauses before his next puff of the pipe. He stands up and throws his blanket off behind him. I've already seen that look on him once before, and it's never good.

"Comanche, what's wrong?" I ask, as he stands over me.

He tosses the pipe overboard. "No more smoke… No more smoke!!" He runs over and pulls the alarm to sound off the entire ship. They go off loudly and the skipper comes out of the wheelhouse instantly.

"What the…" A boat is on fire out in the ocean, maybe about a hundred yards from us, just drifting in flames.

"Comanche, get the dinghy boat ready to be lowered away!!! You, get the rest of those guys up and suit up," yells the skipper from above.

I look at him and then look back at the boat on fire. Where did that boat come from?

"God Dammit! Now, Greenhorn! Move your ass!!!" He yells at me again over the fire alarm.

I hear the engines start up as Comanche runs by me to the back of the boat towards the dinghy. Comanche pulls a cord, and I can hear the dinghy boat inflating as I make my way down to the guys. I'm too late, as they are already rushing up the steps. Scotty hands me another cold suit to put on over my main wet gear.

"We saw it from the window," Diesel says.

Scotty runs over to help Comanche start lowering the dinghy down into the water at the side of the ship. The skipper shuts the alarm off. Now I can hear screaming. It's very faint and sounds like at least two different people are screaming. Not just yelling for help. Screaming in pain and agony.

"Get ya cold suit on, lad. You're going with Diesel out there. I nabbed the first aid box for ya. They need a medic out there. Those people are hurtin'," Scotty says.

Diesel is already in the boat, looking over the motor and pulling on the starter cord. I jump down in with him as Scotty and Comanche lower away.

Skipper comes down to the ship's edge, "Greenhorn," he yells, grabbing my attention. He throws a small, low range walkie talkie to me from the boat. "Tell me everything you see, bring in any survivors, and salvage their radio from that boat before it goes down!!!"

"Hold on, Isaac. This is gonna be fast and bumpy," Diesel says as he gets the engine started and we take off.

I hold the side of the little boat with one hand and keep a death grip on the first aid kit in the other. The tiny boat bounces over the top of even the smallest wave. My cold suit doesn't help me much until I get it fully zipped up the first chance I get. I look behind us and see the ship is getting turned around to head our way. The dinghy moves faster to get to the flaming boat. It's the type that inflates within seconds and you drop the small, but powerful, outboard motor on top of it and it's ready to move. It travels light and fast to get to the burning boat, but not strong or fast enough to go long distances or even with several passengers.

"Talk to me, Greenhorn", says Skipper Walsh over the tiny radio.

I hold the radio up to my face, "We're coming up on the boat now."

Diesel slows us down, but the water stays rippled around the smaller vessel that is up in flames. He circles the boat, looking for any survivors.

"I heard screaming from the ship, man."

"I know. Me too," Diesel says as we look over the burning wreckage.

A side of the boat is tipping over. What's a boat this small doing way out here? Especially a speedboat. Why a speedboat? I recognize those colors. "Slow down!!" I tell him as we get a better look. It's definitely a speedboat, and it has bullet holes all over the side and the small windshield in the front of it. It can't be the same speedboat. That was days ago now. The bullet holes are no coincidence though. Especially the bullet holes that have blood splattered on them.

"Is that what I think it is?" Diesel asks, as he keeps us steered away and circling the speed boat.

"I think so," I say, while I raise the radio up to talk into the mic. "Sea Hellion. It's Greenhorn out here. We're looking at the same speedboat that Yellow Jack was offloaded on a few days ago."

"Any survivors or remains?" Skipper asks.

"Still looking…"

"Can you get to their radio system at all?"

"No, sir… It's up in flames and sinking fast," I tell him.

"Get a rope around the boat, if you can, and we'll get it hooked to the ship when we get there in a few minutes. Try and get those flames out so we can salvage what we can for navigation gear and radio equipment. There could still be people on board, so watch yourself…"

"Roger that."

I look behind us and the ship is still slowly moving this way. The first thing that comes to mind is how many shots they have fired to take out all those men with Uzi machine guns? Even worse is whoever did this to them may also do it to us when they discover that the stolen drugs were left on our ship and not on this speedboat? Except for the looming storm in the distance, there's nothing in sight for miles that could have done this to a small speedboat this recently.

"Holy shit, bro. Get a load of that!" Diesel says with excitement.

He brings the boat to an even slower speed. Floating all over one side of the burning speedboat is cash. Loads and loads of bright Canadian currency all over the place, trying to spread out and away with the choppy waters.

"There's the bag," he yells and points.

One of the same bags Yellow Jack carried on board, filled with money, floats near the speedboat that is starting to bubble down into the ocean. I can see several bricks of cocaine filling the water with white powder around the bag. The amount of money in stacks must be in the hundreds, maybe even thousands. I try to focus and look around the boat for anything that might be of use to us, but the flames are just too hot to save anything. Who did I hear screaming from? If there are no survivors still screaming, then where are their remains?

Diesel brings the dinghy to a stop and I can feel debris from the speedboat hitting the bottom of our boat with every ripple in the ocean. Some hits are hard enough to throw off my balance, but I hold on to the side of the dinghy, still looking for anything in the wreckage. Diesel stands up in the boat and starts tying a rope around his waist.

"What are you doing?"

"I'm gonna get that damn bag. I ain't walking away from this shit show empty handed," he says.

"But what about tying off the boat before it sinks?"

"I don't give two shits 'bout that boat. Them beaners got what they deserved for all I care." And without further thought, he jumps in the frigid waters, so cold they take my breath when his splash hits back at me.

"Dammit, Diesel! Get back in the boat," I yell at him while grabbing the rope end left next to me. I quickly tie it to our boat as he pulls away the slack while he swims out. I watch him. I watch the burning speedboat. I look behind me and scan all around to see our ship still coming this way. A yellow tarp floats near the back of the dinghy I'm in. I take another glimpse at Diesel to see him still swimming towards the bag of money. The burning speedboat is sinking faster and faster now. I rush to look at the yellow tarp behind us and reach over to pull it out of the water. More debris hits the bottom of the small boat again. I pull up the yellow torn material from the water while Diesel shouts in excitement as he swims closer and closer to the bag.

It's a jacket I pulled up from the water, not a tarp. It belonged to Yellow Jack, and it's covered in blood mixed with saltwater on the inside. Only, there are no bullet holes that caused the blood. The jacket is ripped and shredded in several places. If not gunfire, then what the hell did this to him?

"Look at all this dough, Isaac," Diesel says, as he lifts the bag up out of the water and starts to swim back.

The speedboat behind him is now smoldering the flames out and only a small section is above water. Diesel just laughs with his fresh bag of loot in hand. He struggles to swim back with the bag under one arm.

"Help pull me in, Isaac!"

I hesitate at first. The jacket is ripped all to hell with teeth marks all around it. There is no debris heavy enough floating around us to hit the bottom of our boat that hard. There's something in the water out here with us. I look beyond Diesel and the last of the burning speedboat and see a cluster of shark fins are coming up behind him fast.

"Swim, Diesel!!! Swim faster, dammit!!! Don't look back!!!"

I grab the rope he is attached to and start pulling him in. He stops and looks behind him to see more sharks raise their fins behind him.

"Ditch the fucking bag and swim!!!"

He lets the bag go in a panic and swims as fast as he can. I pull the rope with everything I got. My frozen hands feel like they're going to rip open from rope burn, but I don't stop. Diesel screams in between each breath he takes as he paddles closer to me. One shark fin raises in front of him.

"Don't look at it! Just keep swimming, Diesel!!!"

He loses his breath with each scream in terror. "HELP ME!!!"

An agonizing horror fills his face before he is pulled under the water. I try to hold the rope he's attached to with all my grip, but it is pulled out of my hands so fast it shreds the skin down to the meat of my palms. I growl in pain and grab the rope again before all the slack is pulled under, but it's too late. The small dinghy boat is getting pulled around on top of the water like a toy in a bathtub. I look behind, screaming for the ship to be closer, but it only moves at a snail's pace. The rope stops pulling the boat and loosens up. Smaller sharks lift their heads up to snap at the blood that drips from my palms off the side of the boat. I keep trying to pull the rope back in and as long as I can feel weight on it, that means Diesel is still attached to it. The rope becomes easier and easier to pull in. He's swimming up. I see a shape coming up and hope he's still alive.

"My leg!!!" He comes up screaming and jerking around in a frenzy. He reaches for me and I can feel my St. Peter get ripped off my neck. I grab him by his belt and the rope tied to his waist, pulling him in the boat as fast as possible. He keeps screaming and holding onto me. The pain he yells out, the blood all over me and floating in the water. The sharks swimming around biting at the air to give another chomping motion at us both. I lay him on the bottom of the boat and half his inner thigh is missing. It sends streams of blood all over the dinghy. The hand he reaches at me with, while screaming and gargling blood, is mangled and now missing multiple digits. A major bite is across his entire belly, turning his clothes into torn up shreds from the struggle.

"I got you! I got you, buddy!" I try to calm him down, but it's useless. I reach for the short-range radio, covered in Diesel's salty blood. "WE'RE COMING IN," I scream over the radio. I throw it back down next to Diesel as he convulses on the floor of the small boat that fills with his blood.

"Just look at me, Diesel. Just keep looking at me. We're headed back to the ship."

I pull the starter rope on the tiny motor and hit the throttle. I hold his arm with each jolt of the ocean that sends the tiny boat into hard, airborne thrusts. His screams become subdued by the sound of the motor. I look back at the speedboat as its remains finally sink to the watery depths below. I steer the small boat while holding his arm and trying to keep him calm. I can see the rest of the crew at the edge of the ship waving at me in concern. I jerk my arm out of Diesel's grip and reach for the radio again.

I lift the radio up to my face while I look at Diesel, going into shock and his eyes roll white into the back of his head. The crew keeps yelling from the ship as I approach them at full speed.

"OPEN THE TRAWL DOORS," I yell into the radio as I blast by the front of the ship. They see Diesel laying in the boat in a puddle of his own blood. Once I'm beyond the ship, I slow down to get turned around. There's no time to raise him, nor this stupid boat out of the water from the side of the ship. I'm taking this thing in right through the trawl doors. I hit the throttle again. Diesel has stopped reaching for me and is losing consciousness.

"Open the doors… Open the fucking doors, dammit," I whisper to myself. The small boat gets closer and closer. This is either really smart or really dumb. If those doors don't get opened up in the next few seconds...

But they finally open. The crew sits at the rear opening of the ship waiting for me to crash this damn thing right onto the back side of the deck. They lowered a net before we hit the deck. The dinghy boat goes airborne onto the hard surface where the net is pulled in, but I hold Diesel down to keep his head from bouncing around. The engine breaks away from the small boat when we hit back down on the hard wood surface.

The netting brings us to a rough stop, but it was fast thinking on their part. Barrels and some equipment fall over all around me and Diesel in the boat, but the crew works together to move it out of the way quickly.

Skipper yells, "You stupid fuckin' greenhorn! What the hell happened out there?!"

"He was attacked by sharks! He's losing a lot of blood and unconscious," I yell back, while trying to catch my breath. They all stare in shock, the amount of blood on me and all over the bottom of the boat. "We gotta get him inside... Now let's go! Let's go! Get him lifted up!"

Chapter 13 - Paranoia

Comanche carries Diesel on is own all the way down into the slaughterhouse. Blood drips all over the deck, down the stairs to head below, and through the hallways. I rip my belt off and wrap it tight around the top of his thigh to slow the bleeding. His hand is another issue, but not as critical as the bleeding that pours from his inner thigh. Comanche lays him on the table, just as he regains consciousness.

"Get his clothes off!! Take the belt off long enough just to get his pants off," I yell. They all follow me on this one. I don't know how to take all this on at once, so I put each of them on a different effort to stop the bleeding. "Get another belt or a bungee cord from the deck and wrap it around his arm as high as possible to slow down the bleeding, then wrap up the hand."

"I'm cold… I'm so cold," Diesel says, in a low moaning. His lips are turning blue from blood loss.

Scotty hurries back upstairs to grab more cords and the first aid kit that I had left. "Comanche, as soon as you get that shirt off, start taping up any of the bites on his belly!"

We resort to duct tape, the plastic wrap that is used to freeze fish, and the fillet knives we used to clean fish. Luckily, we know everything down here is clean. The skipper just stands in the doorway. Stoned and shaking from being coked out of his mind again.

"We gotta get to the nearest port or he needs to get choppered outta here. Nobody can do any of this here. He's lost too much blood!"

The skipper just stares at me. I grab all of Diesel's bloody clothes and walk over to him. I thrust them at his chest to wake him up from his trance. "I said we gotta get him to a hospital! There's only so much I can do here with what we got!"

"No radio," is all he mutters out of his mouth before dropping the blood-soaked clothes down to the floor and walking away.

"Isaac!!! Get over here, lad. Skip's no use to us. We need you," Scotty yells from across the room. I look at Diesel, staring back at me and clinging to life. I take a deep breath to gather my thoughts. I wipe my forehead with bloody hands. "Tell us what to do, Isaac," Scotty says calmly.

"Ok... Ok..."

His clothes are off, and his mutilated thigh is the biggest issue. Comanche wraps up his hand.

"Be sure you splint those fingers as best as you can before you wrap up his entire hand. Try to clean off the entire area and seal it with gauze," I tell Comanche. "Scotty, get me that staple gun out of the med kit."

The bite marks are gushing blood, darker blood than the rest. His internals may have been punctured, but I have no means to tell. I just gotta get this blood to stop flowing out of him. The bites have, or at least the biggest one, has an eighteen-inch radius. Most of the sharks I saw were smaller, but none of them I saw had a mouth full of teeth that big. Each tooth puncture has to be closed individually. Comanche holds him down from squirming too much as I staple them all shut. He growls in pain with each click of the stapler. He waves his one good hand around to reach at me, but it takes Scotty and Comanche to hold him down. Alcohol is poured everywhere before I get his torso wrapped in a mixture of gauze and plastic wrap.

Now, on to his thigh. Most of the blood is squirting from there, but I gotta take off the belt I used as a tourniquet to see what vein I can close up with this quick clot pad.

"Last one Diesel. I know it's tough, but you gotta hang in there... Guys, you gotta really hold him down this time."

Scotty and Comanche, just as scared and as blood soaked as I am, both shake their heads yes in understanding me. Diesel pants for a deep breath and moans in pain. I reach for the tourniquet once I have all the quick clot pads and gauze ready for a bright red waterfall that's about to come. As soon as I release it, I open up his thigh to see multiple veins and arteries are spewing out all over the table and in my face. I press the pads in place, and he screams in pain.

"It fuckin' burns!!!"

"Comanche, you gotta hold him down yourself! Scotty, I need you over here," I yell over Diesel's grunting and screaming. Scotty comes over and holds the quick cot in place. "Pressure… Lots of pressure! I gotta get one more in place before we wrap." I look up at Comanche, "One more, guys."

I slap it on, and his thrusting frenzy nearly tosses me to the ground. He growls in pain more than just screaming at this point. We hold the quick clots in place and Diesel goes limp again.

"Keep holding those there. Tons of pressure on it now," I tell Scotty. I move up to Diesel's neck, scared we may have just lost him, and look for a pulse. And he is still with us. I look up at Comanche and shake my head yes at him. We all have a sigh of relief knowing Diesel is gonna make it. His thigh is cleaned and wrapped up, but these quick clots will have to come off within the next two days.

We get him cleaned off and all his cuts, punctures, and bites cleaned and dressed properly. Comanche, with all his readily available brute strength, carries Diesel to his bunk. I lift my bunk up and out of the way, so Comanche doesn't have to maneuver around to lay him down.

"I need that leg elevated as best as we can. We gotta keep him warm 'til we get him to the nearest hospital."

Scotty gathers all of our spare blankets to cover him as I get his leg propped up. I check his pulse again and his heartbeat is slow, but it's there. Once Diesel is wrapped up, we stand back and look at each other's blood-soaked clothes in a brief silence. Comanche looks at me and gives a gratifying grin.

Scotty slaps me on the back to knock me out of my state of nervousness, "Ya did it there, young matey. You saved him, Isaac," he says smiling. "You did it," he says again. "Got some ol' grit in ya' blood, don't ya? Think the Navy teach ya all that?"

"I guess so…"

"Ahhh… But doing all that you just did under that kind of pressure, I don't think you can thank the Navy for all that. That takes more than what some uniform training can offer."

"Thanks, Scotty. But we're not in the clear yet, guys. We just stopped the bleeding. We gotta keep a close eye on him and he's gotta get to a hospital. Those bite marks on his backside may have started some internal bleeding or hit his…"

"We will… We will keep a close eye on him. You did good, kid… Ok?" Scotty says again, reassuring me.

I just shake my head and sit on the bunk. I more like collapse down on the bunk behind me. "Those were white sharks that got him. There must have been at least five or six of them out there."

"No sharks like that up here. Not this time of year, if ever."

"Did you see the size of that bite mark? I know what I saw! I was fucking out there pulling him back in the boat, dammit!"

Comanche raises his hand and motions me to calm down. Scotty pats me on the back again. "Alright… Alright."

"I saw Yellow Jack's coat too. Torn to shreds by those same sharks. I don't know what they were shooting at from out of that boat or why all the bullet holes. But everyone that was on that boat is dead. Whether it was machine gun spray or sharks that killed them, I don't know 'cause they're all at the bottom of the Atlantic now."

"Maybe it was a drug deal gone bad when they discovered the captain had shorted them?" Scotty asks.

"No… All the drugs and all the money were still there floating around. That's why Diesel jumped in the water, to get some of it. Whatever those drug smugglers were shooting at made them catch fire or jump in the water, or both. What do you mean there aren't any white sharks here?"

"White sharks, or any shark, this water be too cold for them. They ain't privy to these waters, Isaac. Are you sure that's what you saw?"

"Without a single doubt. But what would have made them jump in the water or shoot their boat all to hell, whether or not they knew if sharks were in these waters this time of year?"

"I don't know, and I don't care to find out. Let's find the skipper, shall we? I don't know what the hell he's thinkin' either, floating around out here waiting out the storm. We gotta head in. Whatever is out there that killed them drug mules is still out there too," Scotty demands.

We all head up to the deck after checking over Diesel one more time. I don't even know what time of day it is now. The storm clouds have covered the horizon. Somehow, the waters are as calm as can be. Comanche runs up the steps to the wheelhouse in front of us and starts pounding on the closed door. There are small mounting holes to look through, but all the lights are off inside the wheelhouse. The engine isn't running, but we can't tell where the skipper is inside. A reflective shine comes from his gun though, then I get a better glimpse of him near the wheel. He crouches down next to a seat on the floor in darkness. His arms are wrapped around his knees, but that pistol still stays in his shaky hands. Comanche knocks on the door harder, but still no response.

"Careful guys. I know he's still snortin' lines. That's the only thing that would make your hands shake like that," I tell them as they stand next to the door.

Scotty moves in front of Comanche and knocks on the door, "Walsh?!?! Walsh open up! We gotta take Diesel in. Greenhorn says we need to get him to a doctor! Walsh?!?"

Nothing. We wait in silence and Scotty holds his head up to the door to listen.

"We wait out the storm... That's what I told you before... We wait it out," Skipper yells through the locked door.

Scotty pounds on the door. "Fuck you, Walsh. FUCK YOU!!! Get out here and be a damn skipper. Fucking wanker coward. Get out here and face me!"

Comanche reaches over to calm Scotty down and pushes him away from the door. I step down, knowing the skipper has barricaded himself in and the cocaine has been in his system long enough to start the paranoia effect. He could be right behind that door, holding his gun up to the back of it thinking we're gonna try to break in. Then he wouldn't think twice about shooting down whoever comes in first. This is too dangerous, and I help pull Scotty away from the door.

"Skipper's not gonna help, Scotty. Just get away from there before he pulls that trigger at random through the door."

We walk back down the steps. The entire deck is covered in blood. The netting and gear are tossed everywhere. We just look around, trying to digest everything. I ruined the dinghy when I crashed into the back of the deck. The engine mounts were destroyed, and the actual engine sits at the end near the trawl doors. There's no way that boat could take all three of us to port, even if the motor could be reattached. Then we would have to face a major storm in the open ocean. We'd never make it anywhere and Diesel wouldn't make the journey.

"We're dragging," Comanche says.

"What?" I ask, and he points to the trawl doors that were left open when the boat crashed in. Nobody noticed we were dragging net when the boat came in. We were all trying to get Diesel to stop bleeding. The net that was dropped to cushion the blow when the dinghy crashed landed is actually the spare net.

"Scotty?" I ask for him and he comes over to look things over.

He pulls the cables and asks, "How long have we been dragging net?"

Comanche and I run to each side and look over the edge of the boat.

"We still have one of the net's otter anchors attached to the boat on this side. Comanche, is the other one attached to your side of the boat too?" I ask, as he looks over the ship. He turns back to us and shakes his head yes. "Scotty, how long have we been dragging a single net?"

"I have no clue matey. It's just draggin' behind us, unopened down in the water. We didn't leave it down there. We stowed everything away after the last haul." He pauses for a second, just as confused as we are about why the net would be dragging and how long it's been in the water. Nobody would have thought to look for it when I crashed the dinghy boat on the deck with Diesel.

"Get her hooked up to the winch line, you two, so we can reel it in."

Comanche and I get the ends pulled in, while Scotty gets behind the crane and winch controls. I give Scotty the thumbs up to reel in. It moves in, slowly, as if it's bringing in a full net of fish. Once the top of the net is in, we hook it up to the crane cables to lift it up over the deck. Comanche and I move some of the netting out of the way and the net starts to raise out of the water. I can't believe what I'm seeing. I don't want it to be real, but it's as real as it gets. There's a hand, a single hand stuck in the net and it's cut clean off at the wrist. We all watch in silence and dismay as more body parts come up with the net now moving above us. Some fish drop and flutter around in the blood pooled up at our feet. A leg falls out first, then a dead seal, and lastly a torso with some limbs still attached. The leg, and anything else not attached, had been cut clean off. The head is still attached, but his face is frozen in a panic and a scream that he died with. All the skin is wrinkled up from being underwater for hours.

Even though it drops to the deck from several feet above, the body and any part that was cut off of him slams down on the deck like a frozen chunk of ice. I look at his arm and see that his hand was cut clean off. A dark and twisted bit of karma has come for our deck boss who we thought had gone missing when all this went to shit for us. Comanche slowly approaches to move some of the netting around to get a better look. I drop to sit on the nearest barrel I can find, ready to throw up on an empty stomach.

"Is it him? Is that Dick?" Scotty asks from behind the crane controls.

Comanche just shakes his head yes and says, "Who done this?"

"Jesus Christ," Scotty mumbles in deep concern.

"I don't think it's a matter of *who* done this?" They both turn to listen to me as I hold my stomach. "It's a question of *what* done this?"

He must have been in the net the entire time since he went missing. Skin is purple and blue in some places. That frozen face is full of wrinkles from the sea water. Crab, fish, and even seal have had a go at him for a piece of a free meal since we started holding the ship in place in the same area since we stopped fishing. There is nothing that can explain this to anyone. Something wants us all to meet our demise in the worst ways imaginable out here. The fear that crosses my mind is wondering if Dick was still alive while his limbs were being chopped off? Did whatever do this allow him to bleed out and die before he was tossed into the nets next to all his limbs? And how did it know to specifically chop off a single hand for what he may have done to the last greenhorn?

Comanche stops bringing in the net, drops it on the bloody deck, and just stares behind us. A cluster of body parts lay sprawled out on the deck full of blood and he looks out to the sea. He doesn't move a muscle. Scotty is doing the same thing. I tell myself not to turn around. I don't want to know what they are looking at in a horrific silence. I don't know how much more I can handle. All I want to do is go home. I turn around to see what they see and my heart sinks. As if the torment of this journey hasn't been enough. A cannon blast into a shipmate my age. Drug smugglers with enough firepower to start a war. A ship captain that hasn't functioned without drugs in his system since we left port, however long ago that was now. Another shipmate nearly eaten alive by white sharks. And now it comes for the rest of us.

"What the hell is that?"

"That be a frozen fog, Isaac," Scotty says with a trembling voice.

"Have you ever seen that before?"

"There be lots of things on this trip I haven't seen before mates. And this is one of them. The unreal is now real and we are not wanted here in these waters."

We all look at this looming fog that's behind the ship. A blind fog that doesn't move or allow any sight beyond it. So dense, it must be "frozen", as Scotty says. We just drift around between two vast amounts of dread and doom. To one side of us, in the distance, is a fog that can hide anything within the known and unknown world that brings us to our deepest fears. On the other side, closing the distance to us, is a storm that can cripple the natural world of all hope. Reminding us all that nature was God's remedy to cleanse the world of all of us. Both entities, whether it be the fog on one side or the storm on the other, slowly loom closer to our lowly vessel in the several minutes we stand there and gaze at it. We gaze at both demises heading our way, not in awe, but in a fear of its purest form. Fear of the deadliest unknown.

"We have to take the ship…"

Scotty and Comanche turn around and look at me, "What?" Scotty says.

"You heard me. I don't care about the drugs or the money, or the skipper. Diesel is down below, and he might die. How many more of us have to die out here? There's something out there in either direction that is after us. This isn't about getting out of this ahead or rich anymore. This is about surviving."

Scotty looks up at Comanche. Comanche lowers his head for a sec, he takes a deep breath into that large barrel chest of his, lifts his head and nods yes at Scotty.

They both stare in silence for a moment before Scotty opens up again. "Alright then, lads… We take the ship."

Chapter 14 - The Mutiny

The duffle bag that has all that remains of our deck boss is placed next to Iceman in the freezer. We did our best to piece him back together, but none of us realized how stiff his limbs and joints would be. I'm sure we heard bones crack when Comanche put some weight down onto the duffel so we could zip it up. None of us had any kind words to say about him, despite his brutal demise. The only questions we discuss was "who did this and how it went unnoticed?" The major questions not spoken was if there was a potential that it isn't a *who* at all that may have done this, but more like a *what* may have done this? It could have been easily played off on the skipper's part when he came down to ask us where Dick was the same day he went missing. He has everything to gain by none of us making it home alive. Thus, making him the main suspect here. But if that were the case, why no screams when he was cut all to hell? Why no noise when the single net was lowered? It's not like the trawl door on the deck is quiet either in its rickety age. Another farfetched culprit is not knowing if there is a murderous drug mule on board hiding somewhere just to pick us off one by one for the skipper skimming them off the top.

I really don't think any of that's the case, though. It's just the things that we all question each other with to avoid discussing the idea that something else could be among us. If seeing is believing, then I know what I saw. An unreal storm to one side, and an unreal fog on the other. But somewhere on board is an omen of terror. With or without her head falling off of her depends on the time, apparently. I haven't seen her since the lightning strike. It is apparent that she is only appearing when the visibility is limited. Of all the things that have happened, this is what lurks in my mind. With the coming darkness and a looming fog of ice, nobody would see her coming if this she-ghost was behind all this mental torture. Torture for someone else's wrongdoing that we all now suffer for. I go to close the freezer doors and see the lump-filled duffle bag of him, bulging in various places, next to Iceman who remains neatly packed and wrapped for safekeeping until proper burial. I can only hope we can make it back to do so, but that hope is fading by the hour.

"Go check on Diesel for me, Isaac," Scotty says.

I make my way to the bunk room up from the slaughterhouse and he's already awake. Before I talk to him, I run back to the kitchen for a bottle of water. Comanche is already in the room when I come back, and I see Scotty making his way down the corridor.

"Here... Drink this for me," I tell Diesel, as I kneel next to his bunk. Comanche holds his head up and he coughs with the first few sips. He shakes his head to have us move the water away. "Ok... How do you feel, Diesel?"

"I'm just cold, man... Freezing cold."

I put my hand on his sweating forehead and he is, without a doubt, running a fever. Comanche reaches for more blankets, but I motion him to hold off. "I know you're trying to help, big guy, but I gotta check his wounds first before we get him warmed back up. Scotty, do we have any fever reducer or ibuprofen back in the medical kit? Maybe in the mess?"

"I'm on it," he says and walks out the room.

"Comanche, help me lift him up for a bit..."

I uncover him and guide Comanche to slowly lift him. Diesel groans in pain, but I see his bandages are clean covering his bite marks on the torso. We lower him back down slowly, then I move to his hand. Scotty comes back with everything he can find and gives Diesel some meds while I re-bandage his hand. Most of his fingers are going gray in color. The blood has stopped flowing, but an infection is spreading from the digits he's missing. I get them covered up before he has a chance to see them for himself. Then I have Comanche lift his leg up to check the bite mark on his thigh.

"How is it?" Diesel asks, while struggling in the throbbing pain.

I don't know what to do other than divert his attention and keep him positive. "You lost some serious blood, but we got the bleeding to stop. Now your body has to recuperate fresh blood. That's why you're so cold. So, no jackin' it off with your good hand for a few days, alright?" I smile at him.

He tries to laugh but converts to a struggled cough. "I need to see you," I tell Scotty. "Comanche, you can get him warmed up like you were about to do, please."

Comanche gets more blankets on top of him while Scotty and I step out into the hallway.

"How bad is the lad?" Scotty asks.

"It's his thigh. That's the worst one. We gotta keep that fever under control, but we need antibiotics to fight that infection. With arterial bleeding like that, if an infection gets potent enough and into his bloodstream, no amount of painkillers in the world will stop his heart from giving out."

"How long do we have?"

"Two... Three days max. I don't know. Once those bandages come off with that quick clot, it could drain out some of the infection. But then he loses more blood, and we have to stop the blood flow all over again. He needs something beyond what I can do with what we got on this ship. We'll be resorting to duct tape and Saran Wrap again before you know it. We need to get him to a hospital."

"Port is days away," Scotty says with a sigh.

"Not if we just push right into Canada. Forget heading stateside. Steam right into Newfoundland and the first boat we see, we just start sending up flares so they can call for help on the radio and get Diesel choppered out of here. We couldn't do that for Iceman, but it's the least we can do for Diesel. The longer we wait on this, the less time he has. Scotty, I'm with you on this, but we gotta do it soon."

"Alright Isaac. Let's go tell him what's going on, then, lad."

We walk back in and Scotty doesn't waste a second. He leans down next to Diesel. "We're takin' the ship, matey. We gotta get you choppered outta here and the rest of us back to port before the drug mules get the rest of us."

"The rest of us?" Diesel asks tirelessly.

Scotty looks up at me and Comanche. I just shake my head and let him know what we've discovered, since he's been bedridden for the last several hours. "The skipper's cracked out of his mind and locked himself in the wheelhouse, and Dick is dead. We found him being dragged in the net. We don't know how long since he drowned."

Comanche and I don't bother to correct Scotty on that. Only the three of us need to know that he was chopped in several pieces, more than likely before he drowned.

"Are you going to the port authorities and tell them about what happened?" Diesel asks.

Scotty hesitates on how to answer that. If it were me, I would say *yes* without hesitation, but I'm leery of why he paused before answering him.

"What's most important is that we get you to a hospital for proper care," he tells him. "And we're taking the ship. We gotta get you outta here and save our asses before these drug mules come looking for this ship. And they'll be coming with a lot more firepower this time. Especially knowing how much damage they did to one of their own on that speedboat that had Yellow Jack in it."

Diesel just shakes his head yes and his eyes become heavy. Scotty turns around, "Alright lads. Any plans on how we pull this off without getting shot to hell and back?"

Scotty and I sit on one of the bunks together and we lower our voice. Comanche stands by the door just in case, keeping an eye out for the skipper.

"He's only got the one gun, right?"

"As far as I know," Scotty says. I look at Diesel and Comanche and they both shake their heads yes.

"I think it's a 1911 style forty-five. So, that means he can only shoot about seven or eight rounds before reloading. If we can get him to unload at us until empty, then we can jump him. We just need him to come out of the wheelhouse before he reloads. If he even has another loaded magazine to go with that gun."

Scotty just looks at me in shock. "So, we just let him take a shot at us, seven or eight times. Hope that he misses each of us with every shot. And then jump him. Is that how they do things in the Navy?"

"Ya know, I'm the only one coming up with any ideas here. It's not like we train for this type of shit."

"So, what do you guys do then? Just float around in the ocean until some war starts?"

"Yeah… Pretty much… Smart ass."

"You draw him out," Diesel interrupts as Scotty and I argue. "Kill the lights and he'll come out looking for why he's in the dark. Kill the main power for the wheelhouse down in the engine room and he'll come out expecting one of you guys to fix it."

Comanche shakes his head yes.

"Well, mates. That solves how to draw him out. But how do we solve the problem of *not* getting shot up on deck?" Scotty asks.

"We shield ourselves from the bullets. What do we have that can take several forty-five rounds and not get through?"

"Slaughterhouse," Comanche says.

"That's right…" The good idea fills my head. "The wooden butcher tables down in the slaughterhouse, and all those other stainless-steel tables on top. That will stop anything he shoots at us. The countertop tables in the kitchen too."

"Well," Scotty thinks out loud. "It only takes one person to shut down the main power. But as soon as that happens, the other two have to be ready right by the wheelhouse door with these shields to jump him. Maybe this can be done without a single shot fired. Then we can steam to the nearest port. Signal any boat that comes near us and get Diesel out of here sooner."

"Then we tell the port authority everything," I add in.

"Right…" There's that pause again from Scotty. "Then we tell them everything that's happened… Right. That's it then, lads. So, who's gonna kill the power and be in the dark while the other two risk eating a bullet?"

We all stay silent. I have no interest in going into the engine room and fumbling around in the dark, clueless as to what's going on up on deck.

"At this point, I'd rather face a loaded gun then to see her again in the dark."

"This whispering widow shit again… Come on, Isaac." Scotty raises his hands in contempt.

I push him off the bunk next to me. We both stand up in each other's face, "I know what I fuckin' saw. And don't act like you don't believe me when I know you and Comanche knew what I was talkin' about, dammit. There's something on this ship!"

Comanche stands in between us, but Scotty keeps going at it with me, "Oh… Just like them great white sharks you claim you saw eatin' him alive!"

"It was great whites," Diesel says. We all stop our bickering and look at him. "I know it's crazy, but he's right. The water is way too cold for them to be all the way up here this time of year. Those were great whites."

"White shark don't hunt in packs," Scotty argues more.

"These ones do. They weren't tigers or bull sharks. They were whites. And I got a lot closer than any of you ever did. When Isaac says they were white sharks, you best listen to him."

"Fine…" Scotty continues, "I'm not going down to the engine room. You are kid." Pointing at me. "And

I want my stab at the skipper more than anyone else on the ship. And Comanche, I need your size to rush him and pin him down. Are we all on the same page?"

We all shake our heads again before he continues. "Alrighty... Diesel, I need you to stay awake long enough to tell Isaac here what to do as far as shutting down the ship. Isaac, you make sure he's good to go for a bit while we pull this one out of our ass. Comanche, you and me are going down to the slaughterhouse to rip up some tables and butcher block. We meet back at the door to take us on deck as soon as we can. Alrighty then, lads?"

Scotty and Comanche break away. I turn to Diesel, who's half-conscious again. I lightly shake him, and he comes to.

"It's very simple, Isaac," he says as his eyes roll around a bit. "You go all the way to the back side of the engine room between the two main engines. You'll find the main circuit board for the entire ship and it will be attached to a back-up generator."

"Ok?"

"You just pull the lever for main power down and everything shuts off. Engines, lights, everything shuts down," he says.

"Wait... That's it?"

"Yeah. That's it."

Diesel starts to close his eyes again, but I tap his shoulder anyway. "Are you sure, Diesel? It can't be that simple, can it? Isn't there like a full-on process to go through, or?"

"Bro… We're simple seamen on a fishing boat. What do they do to you Navy boys to make you guys overthink shit and make everything so complicated? Yes… It really is that simple… Can I go back to sleep now?"

Chapter 15 - Taking the Ship

I leave Diesel to go back to sleep after I get him to take some more meds. Comanche comes back, muscling the entire butcher-block table. They took the legs off the stainless-steel table too and resorted to duct taping the two tables together. With the way Comanche struggles to carry the combined tables through the hallway, it must be at least a hundred pounds. Scotty comes up from behind with one of the table legs in hand and a fillet knife in the other. He hands over a flashlight to me and keeps one for himself. One of the many rolls of duct tape they used to put the tables together is attached to his belt on the back side.

"Come with me lad," Scotty waves me out into the hallway. "Your gonna sneak out on deck first and I want you to get one of the life rafts available on the deck somewhere. Me and Comanche are gonna get up to the wheelhouse door, but don't head down to the engine room 'til I give you the signal. As soon as the lights are out, you come back out on deck to make sure we didn't get ourselves killed."

"But why am I getting a life raft ready?"

"Well… 'Cause if me or Comanche go down, you can bet he'll kill anybody else on the ship. You, me, Comanche, and Diesel too. He won't risk anymore incidents. If things go wrong, you sneak out and jump ship with the life raft. Pull the string to blow it up and paddle 'til you can't paddle no more. You push into that fog, then hope he won't be able to find you. All those life rafts have flare guns, but don't use it 'til you can get to another boat safely, Aye?"

I shake my head yes and close the door to the bunk room. We make our way to the deck. Comanche uses all his strength to bring their makeshift shield on the deck without bumping into anything. I quietly step around on the dark ship deck. I look up to keep an eye out on the wheelhouse, but luckily, most of the windows that oversee the deck from the wheelhouse are boarded up. I try not to remind myself how much I dread being in the dark on this ship. But it's the only thing I can think about now that I'm trying with every movement to stay out of any light I see. The life raft is closer to the rear trawl doors, but I unattached it and leave it loosely strapped to the railing at the ship's edge. I come back and wait by the door that leads down to the engine room but stay low into the shadow created by the accent lights of the stairs leading up to the wheelhouse.

I have a clear visual of Comanche and see Scotty trailing right behind him. They slowly make their way up the stairs to the wheelhouse. They get right next to the wheelhouse door and Comanche lifts their shield up, stressing to not make a noise with the weight of the table. All is quiet while they both catch their breath. A chilling breeze passes through the ship as I wait for Scotty's signal that they are in place. They whisper something to each other, and Comanche shakes his head yes. Scotty gives the thumbs up and I turn around to head down into the only part of the ship I haven't been in often enough to get familiar with, the engine room.

I stumble around in the darkness. My heart can't keep up with my breathing, or maybe it's the other way around. I glide my hands over the walls to look for a light switch, and the rumble of the engines is deafening. I can only imagine the noise when they are at full speed. The skipper has kept us in the same position for a few days now and the effort to save fuel is critical. I find the light switch and discover that only one engine is running, which makes sense if we aren't moving very far. Pipes and cables run throughout the loud room, it's hard to imagine more than one person down here attempting to maintain all this. But Diesel is correct.

Right in between the two main ship engines is the main control panel. It even has a piece of tape on it with an arrow that says *main power* next to the lever. Maybe it is just my military mindset overcomplicating things, but I waste no more time in questioning a good thing. I drop the lever and the engines shut down. They spin at a slow idle for a bit and finally slow to a stop. Everything has gone freakishly dark and to a deadly silence down here in the most claustrophobic room on the ship.

Scotty would give me the one flashlight with the batteries almost dead. A few new bumps to the head and I make my way up to the deck. My eyes adjust and I still see Scotty and Comanche waiting outside the door. There is movement inside the wheelhouse. The skipper may be checking things on his end as to why he's lost all power. We wait for several seconds that feel like an eternity. Then a flashlight comes on in the wheelhouse. Scotty and Comanche prepare for the worst in running the skipper down with a table for a shield. I stay low near the engine bay stairwell door and helplessly wait, even holding my breath while staying low in the ship's darkness. The only light is the tiny flashlight the skipper holds as he approaches the door of the wheelhouse. It slowly opens…

"Get him!!!" Scotty yells.

Comanche rushes forward and pins the skipper up against the doorway. The struggle they all go through is hard to see, but no shots are fired.

"You fuckin'," exclaims the skipper, as he pushes back against the table that Comanche forces against him with all his strength. I run up to them to help, but I can see the skipper is reaching for his gun lodged in his belt. Scotty and Comanche still struggle to get him down to the floor with the table on top of him. Scotty grabs the skipper's free hand on the other side of the table shield. The skipper grunts and thrusts around with all the adrenaline and drugs running through his system. I make it up to them, in time to see the unbelievable amount of force Comanche has to use to hold down the skipper. They kicked the flashlights around in the wheelhouse, but a reflection of light comes from the gun the skipper has managed to get to with his free hand.

"Bang!!... Bang!!..."

"Holly shit!" A bullet gets lodged in the doorway that I was about to run through. Skipper jerks his arm with the gun around to point it at Comanche, holding him down with all his weight on the table shield. Scotty still struggles with the skipper's other arm and doesn't see that Skipper has freed the gun from under Comanche's weight.

"Bang!!... Bang!!... Bang!!..."

The gun shots ring through my ears and turn me deaf. I can't even hear the skipper fighting them back in panic. Every shot has been aimed at Comanche, holding him down with the table shield. The skipper grinds his teeth, and I can see him attempting to turn the gun back at him. Comanche's eyes go wide in the struggle and attempts to free a hand to reach for the gun while holding the skipper down at the same time. Skipper forces his wrist to turn the gun at Comanche. Without a second thought, I lunge to the floor and grab Skipper's arm while trying not to point the gun at myself. His sure grip on the gun is not budging.

"Bang!!…"

I don't know how many shots that was, but it bounces off the floor, barely missing my leg and bounces through one of the boarded windows. The recoil of the last shot loosens the skipper's grip and I pry it from his hand as he keeps pulling the trigger, but the hammer drops on my thumb.

"I got it!!! I got the gun!" I yell.

The skin fold of my thumb is cut open. I have to pry the hammer out of it before I try to cock it back in place. I turn to point it at the skipper as Comanche lifts up the tables. But the skipper just forcefully pushes the tables off himself and they land on my legs. Skipper's eyes are wide open and bloodshot as sweat pours from his hair line over his freshly bruised face. I quickly scurry out from under the table. He sees me holding the gun as I tamper with the hammer again to pull it back. His breathing is rapid, and I didn't notice the bricks of cocaine that are open when I jumped down to help Comanche in the struggle. He lunges at me like a crazed lunatic. He yells something, but I can't hear through the ringing in my ears. Before he has a chance to have a go at me, Scotty bashes him in the head from behind with the table leg. The skipper drops to the ground, but still attempts to crawl closer to me, still growling, baring his teeth, and yelling something in his crazed state of near overdose on too many lines of coke. Scotty hits him in the back of the head again, and he drops unconscious a few inches away from me, still reaching for the loaded gun in my hand.

Scotty goes to hit him again in the back of the head while he lay on the floor passed out, but Comanche stops him. I just sit there on my ass with my back against the doorway, nervously holding the gun aimed at the skipper as blood starts to fall from the back of his head. His arms are cut up in multiple places, but that didn't happen in the effort to subdue him. Those cuts are recent, but not from our struggle just now. He's been doing enough drugs and has stayed locked in this room long enough to start mutilating himself with a fillet knife. I slowly drop the hammer on the gun and reach for his neck to look for a pulse.

"He's still alive."

We all look around the room in shock. Shock from getting shot at and still living to talk about it. But we gaze in horror from the drawings all over the back side of the boarded-up windows. The skipper has completely lost his mind, staying up here alone and taking in every line of cocaine he could. None of the drawings or words make sense. It's just a jumbled mess of madness written in his own blood from the last few days.

"Get him tied up with the tape in case he wakes up." I tell them, as the ringing in my ears weaken.

Scotty pulls out the tape attached to his belt and pulls the limp arms of the skipper to his backside to tape them together. He wraps the tape around a dozen times while trying to catch his breath. Comanche gets on his feet and walks over to help me stand up. He looks at me and shakes his head in thanks for saving him from a shot to the head.

"I guess we're even now, yeah?" He shakes his head again, with a grin this time.

Scotty works on binding the skipper's legs together, then looks at his own hands. His own hands are covered in blood.

"Scotty, did you get hit? Are you shot?"

He shakes his head no, "That's not my blood... That's the skipper's. His wrists are covered in his own blood."

Comanche and Scotty both turn to look at the radio. The ringing in my ears is still there but faded low enough to hear what's coming through the radio. The same scratchy violin tune. I step over the skipper, who's still passed out, to get closer to the speaker. I hear the broken and eerie violin repeatedly trying to stroke a tune.

"Did he get the radio fixed and not tell us?" I ask.

Scotty reached behind the radio to show that the power cord and other various wires are still fried up from the lightning strike. Scotty just looks at us and shakes his head no.

Comanche walks to the wheelhouse exit and stops dead in his tracks.

"Guys," he says as he looks at the door. He turns to look at us, then turns back to look at the door again before closing it. He turns on another flashlight and points at the door. The inside of the door is covered in more blood. More scribbled words written in the blood of a crazed skipper in his delusional state of cocaine use.

It says... *I die. Chaleur take me. I die... Chaleur take me. I die...*

It's all over the inside of the door. Repeated again and again in blood. We look around the room and see the resemblance of the same thing written on the tables, the boarded-up windows, and the walls. They all have the same things written on them. Only several of the attempts of writing in blood have dripped down to make it hard to read.

"Jesus… Another day of losing this much blood and he would have just woke up dead."

"Not unless that's Dick's blood when he chopped him up and threw him in the net," Scotty replies.

Forgetting that the broken radio still brings in that scratchy violin tune, Comanche walks past us both and rips it off the table. He steps over the skipper and walks out the wheelhouse door while saying nothing to either of us. Outside the wheelhouse, Comanche throws the radio overboard into the cold black sea. The violin coming through the radio fades out as it slowly takes in water and sinks to the depths below. Comanche just watches from over the rails to make sure it sinks below the water until we hear the violin no more.

"He went mad up here, lads," Scotty says, still looking around the blood-soaked room in disgust and confusion. "How in the living hell is he even alive?" He shakes his head, trying to get the imagery out of his mind and gets Comanche's attention. "Comanche… Go down below and turn the power back on." He shakes his head yes, looks over the rail once more to make sure the radio sank, and heads down the stairs.

Scotty walks over to me with his hand out. He points at the gun that I forgot I was still holding. I back away from him in concern, and he holds both hands up to ease my tension. "It's alright, Isaac. I'm not gonna hurt you. We're headed home. Alright lad," he says, while reaching for the gun slowly again. "We're headed home, Isaac. Trust me, mate." I hand him the gun, but I'm ultimately ready to drop back down to the floor again. Everything has caught up with me. The lack of sleep. The gunfire. The shark attack on Diesel. Iceman reaching for life. It all hits me in flashbacks. The blood all over the wall. It's all sinking in and I can't breathe while leaning over.

"Get up Isaac. We're not out of this yet." Scotty says, while helping me get back up. "Snap out of it, lad. We're headed home, but we're not outta this yet." I shake my head, trying to stay focused. "I want you to head down and check on Diesel. You have to tend to him. Let him know we have the ship. Aye?"

"Who is *Chaleur*?" I ask as he tries to bring me back to a state of reality.

"It don't matter. He went mad up here, Isaac. You know that. Now go tend to Diesel like I asked you to."

"Don't bullshit me. I saw the look on Comanche's face when he saw what was written in blood. Now who is *Chaleur*?"

He pauses for a sec and bends down, while stuffing the gun in his own belt, to look over the skipper who still lays unconscious. He looks up at me and sighs. "It's not a who. It's a what. And it's the name of the ship I told you about. It's just an old sea story, nothing more."

"It's more than just an old sea story to Comanche and obviously the captain too."

He stands back up when the power of the wheelhouse comes back on. The lights flicker and several of the control panels blink on with various lights. He steps back over the skipper and goes to look over the controls.

Not set at ease with his answer and ignoring me more, I walk over to him and thrust him around by the arm.

"I told you. It's the name of a ship," he says as he jerks my hands off his elbow. "It's a pirate ship full of the dead. It comes with sails of fire as it burns all in its path."

"But you said it's just a story."

He turns back around to the control panel and presses the switch to get the motors back on. "I hope so, lad. I hope it is just one of those sea stories we hear being out here long enough. But I don't care to stick around here anymore to find out that it's *not* just a story…"

Chapter 16 - Adrift

"Diesel... Diesel..." I gently shake him and notice right away he is sweating profusely from fever. He comes to and rolls his eyes around a bit before focusing in on me. "How you feelin' buddy?"

"I'm just cold, bro... And thirsty."

I get up and grab a bottle of warm water from the mess. He barely sits up to be able to drink anything. He coughs and spits some out in his struggle, but he still gets some. That's when I notice his eyes have a yellow tint and are bloodshot. He lays his head back down.

"I gotta check over some of these bandages, alright?"

"Are we headed home?" he asks while his eyes start to close again.

"Yeah man... We have the ship. We're headed back now. We tied the skipper up in the wheelhouse."

He just shakes his head while I look over his hand. I take off all the blood-soaked wraps and gauze to see his mangled hand with missing fingers. The bleeding there has stopped, but he needs more stitches than I can offer. Maybe even a surgery to repair the muscle and tendon tissue to salvage what they can. I uncover him more to look at the major bites on his torso. The bandages are still bloody, and he struggles to turn over to his uninjured side so I can remove them and put fresh ones on. Dark brown and yellow puss drools from each puncture wound from shark teeth. But again, the bleeding has stopped. The concern now is keeping it clean and making sure any infection puss can be drained and cleaned out.

The inner thigh bite is the worst of all of them. As soon as I cover his torso back up with the blanket and uncover his leg, the smell hits my nostrils like rotten eggs. He coughs again, and the overabundance of bandages wrapped around his thigh still tries to soak up blood that keeps oozing. The bleeding has slowed down, but I really can't tell if it's more blood or infection bile trying to drain out from his thigh. The more bandages I uncover, the more yellow, green, and brown they become, the closer I get to the actual bite wound. The smell fills through the room, but I hold my gag down by resorting to a fake dry cough.

"Can you take that quick clot off? It burns," he asks.

I don't know what to tell him, if I should tell him anything at all. His leg is totally brown, black, and blue. The infection has gone to his lower foot, and the veins show that it's traveling back up the leg too. I've seen nothing on this level of horrid as far as an injury on the Naval carriers. Bumped heads, shattered knees, and hurt feelings mostly. "I can't do that for you right now. We gotta leave that in for the pros at an ER station when we get back to port. The plan is, if we see a ship, we flag it down so we can radio in for help to get you airlifted outta here." I reach down and lightly prick several areas of his foot and toes with the ends of a pair of scissors in the med kit. "Tell me, can you feel any of that?"

He just shakes his head no. "Feel what?" he asks in a low mumble.

My heart sinks for him. I look at him and listen to him wheezing as he slowly drifts back to sleep. I replace what bandages I can for his leg before covering him back up. We gotta get him back before he loses this leg. Or even worse, the infection spreads more than it already has. He's already had enough medication to overwork his liver and kidneys. I sit with him for a while as he comes in and out of his fever induced sleepiness. I check his pulse and his heart rate is ridiculously high for someone going in and out of sleep. Sepsis is a near fatal infection, whether viral or bacterial from the shark bite doesn't matter. This can be deadly.

I've been down here in the bunk house with him for at least an hour, but the ship still isn't moving much. The engines are just above idle to keep the ship in place against the current. I look over Diesel one last time before I head up to the deck. The morning haze is coming in and that fog is closer than ever. The wind keeps bringing it closer to the ship and I hope Scotty up in the wheelhouse has realized this. I look over towards home and a pattern of dark and dreary storm clouds still surrounds it. How the sea remains calm in this small corridor between two harsh weather patterns may baffle even the most honest of meteorologists, if there is such a thing anymore.

Yelling and commotion come from the wheelhouse as I gaze at the storm in the distance. "You fuckin' bastards don't know what you've done!!!" That's the skipper raising hell with Comanche and Scotty up there with him. He must have woken up from that hit Scotty gave him on the back of the head. I head up to the wheelhouse, but the door slams open. The skipper is jerking and fidgeting around with his hands tied behind his back. Comanche carries him over one shoulder, keeping him in place with one arm. "Put me down you fucking ape!!!" he yells in Comanche's ear. I quickly hurry back down the steps before I get in Comanche's way and Scotty follows right behind him with that pistol in hand.

Once on the deck level, Comanche throws Skipper down on the hard floor. Knocking over several buoys and rigging equipment. The skipper grunts from his harsh landing in front of me, but he can't get back on his feet while still being tied up. He has several fresh bruises and marks from a recent beating to his face. But the crazed stare he looks up at me with as he lay on the deck floor gives me enough detail to know he is still under an adrenaline rush from a near cocaine overdose. His wrists are bleeding again from his self-mutilation. But why would Comanche and Scotty be giving him a beat-down while tied up?

"What the hell's going on? Why aren't we heading back?" I ask frantically and confused.

"Fetch the life raft, Comanche," Scotty says. "You'll want no part in this, Isaac. Stay below and tend to Diesel just as you were told, lad."

"Hell no... What have you two done to him? What is going on?"

Comanche comes back from the other side of the deck with the same life raft that I stashed aside before we took the ship. He pulls the cord, and it blows up in a matter of seconds in front of us on the deck.

"Mutiny is a federal offense you fuckin' pukes!!!" Skipper yells, as he still squirms around, tied up. His blood still flows from the back of his head.

"So is trafficking drugs across international waters. You'll see to it that we all end up in the brig with you, no matter what port we make it to," Scotty replies.

I rush over to Comanche, checking over the life raft. He pulls out the paddle, along with the emergency bag that houses flares and a few rations, then tosses it to the other side of the deck. All that's left in the tiny life raft, maybe four feet around, is a single rope.

"Comanche... What are you doing?"

But he ignores me and ties the raft with the rope. He lifts it up and throws it over the side of the ship, holding on to the rope as it falls into the water.

"They're after you and the drugs, Walsh. Not us or the ship," Scotty says.

Comanche ties off the life raft to the side of the ship then heads back up to the wheelhouse. The skipper looks more terrified than full of adrenaline now, as if he knows what's about to happen, but I can't fathom any of this in my mind.

"Scotty. We can't do this. We just can't. We gotta take him into the authorities. Jesus, man. We have the ship. Just keep him tied up and we can tell them everything." I plead with Scotty. But he doesn't listen. He just keeps that gun pointed at the skipper. Comanche comes back down with a single duffle. White powder poofs into the air and spreads from the zippers. Comanche reaches the bag over the side of the ship, making sure the skipper can see him.

"I come for fish… Not drugs…" Then he drops it down and I can hear it landing in the life raft.

"Stand him up," Scotty says to Comanche. He pulls a fillet knife out from his back side.

Comanche gets the skipper stood up and I rush to get in between them.

"Scotty don't do this. Whatever it is you're about to do, it's not worth it anymore. Diesel is down there dying on us and we gotta get him back. We can deal with the skipper another time."

He looks right at me with the knife in one hand and the gun in the other. "There's been enough death spawned from this man's doing, mate. Step aside, as this is going to happen with or without you, Isaac. Don't make me point this at you too if you're with the skipper. 'Cause he ain't my skipper no more. Trust me when I tell you that this is the way of the sea."

"I told you, you stupid ol' fuckin' seadog! I didn't kill anybody! I don't know who killed Dick or what got Iceman!!!" His rant is interrupted by a slap on the back of the head by Comanche's fiercely large hand.

"This is wrong," I tell them.

Scotty looks down. "It's not about right or wrong. It's about survival. His drug mules are after him. Not us…"

I turn around and look at Comanche. Still straight faced as always and he just shakes his head yes with what Scotty was telling me. I look away and slowly step aside.

"Turn him around," Scotty says to Comanche. The skipper's eyes are as wide and fearful as can be, but he almost tears up when looking at Comanche. Scotty stuffs the pistol in his belt and bends down to cut the tape around his feet, then his hands. Comanche turns him around to face Scotty again, now pointing the gun back at the skipper's head as they square off, face to face.

"This is the end for you Walsh," Scotty tells him.

The skipper quickly snorts his nose and spits at Scotty's face.

Without a second thought, Comanche grabs him and throws him over the side of the ship into the water. We all look over the side of the ship to watch him struggle to swim and get on the raft. The water is a deep, frigid cold that sobers him up and makes him shiver from head to toe. His blood-filled hands and wrists turn the dark blue and gray waters at the ship's edge a bright red. But we weren't the only ones waiting for a decent meal as this nightmarish seafaring journey comes to an end. In the distance are white flutters of water from shark fins closing in. I don't know if the skipper knows that, but he wastes no time getting inside the raft. Just in time to see Comanche untie the rope from the railing of the side of the ship. His raft starts to inch away from the ship. He throws the rope up in a panic, attempting to lasso to the side of the ship before he drifts away.

"You're all gonna burn!!!! YOU'RE ALL GONNA FUCKIN' BURN OUT HERE!!! She's comin'… She's comin' for all of us and you're gonna BURN!!!"

His rants of hatred are interrupted again by what we all know is bumping the bottom of his only life source and protection from the inevitable. Several white sharks circle around the blood that surrounds the raft. They poke their heads out of the water, biting at the cold air with teeth that send chills down my spine. He uses the rope to swing at them.

Scotty pulls out the pistol and drops the magazine. He opens the slide to see one round still in the chamber. He uses his thumb to force out the last round in the magazine and then drops the round down into the ocean, never again to be found or used for whatever vile reason man has to offer. He drops the now empty magazine into the water too, and everything sinks out of sight.

"Fuck you Scotty!!! You're gonna burn like the rest of them!!!" Skipper yells.

Before he gets too far away from the ship with the current, the old 1911 style pistol with a single round left in the chamber is tossed down to land into the life raft. Skipper ignores the sharks, still nudging at his life raft, and quickly reaches for the gun. Such immense amounts of anger fill his eyes turning to tears as he points the gun at us with shaky hands. None of us on the ship budges as the skipper, still slowly inching away from us with the current, considers using his single round to end one of us.

He turns and points the gun at his forehead.

He closes his eyes and tries to scream, but his voice is gone.

It's just a mere scratchy groan from a voice box already broken from cursing at all of us still on the ship, just watching him fade away.

Then it finally comes…

The scream of a broken man that knows his end will be followed by a Hell he hoped wasn't truly real until that time came for him.

He lowers the gun and his head, exhausted from the days of struggle and drug use. He just watches all of us in that continued hatred as the fog consumes him. His tiny life raft is still being bumped and nudged by the ocean's top predators that may only be here this time of year to bring an end to everyone on the ship, in some way or another. There is no wind, no matter how bitterly cold the morning is, that can match the emptiness that now fills me on the inside, in knowing that blood is now on my hands, in sending another man to meet his demise. Even if only to send him to that end adrift on a tiny raft filled with his beloved drugs that set all this turmoil in motion. All along with a single shot left in his own pistol.

Will it be the gun to his head…?

Will it be the ocean that takes him…?

Or could it be what lies within the fog…?

What will take him from this world to the Hell that awaits him in the next? None of us know. All we know is that one of those things will take him. Maybe we say nothing to each other as the freezing fog engulfs the tiny raft, because we know the same may come for us soon enough. We sit and quietly watch until we can't see our former skipper anymore.

"Comanche… Be a lad for me and go up and rev those engines beyond idle speeds. When they ask, we'll say he threw himself over with a life raft to save his own hide and drug stash. Let's go home, boys," Scotty says with a bit of remorse in his voice.

Comanche pauses for a sec, then commits to heading up to the wheelhouse to start the second engine so we can steam home.

But he pauses again before heading up when he hears me say, "We're no better than he is…"

"Why would you say that, aye?" Scotty says with confusion.

I turn to look directly at Scotty, "You may have thrown the gun over. You may have thrown the drugs over too… But you never threw that money over, did you?"

We all just stare at each other. Nobody answers the question. "Like I said, we're no better than he is in all this. And we all know it."

Scotty looks down, then looks out to the freezing misty fog that has consumed the skipper. He turns around to commit to revving up the ship himself and trudges up the stairs to the wheelhouse with his head hung low.

BANG!!!

From a distance, the single round has gone off. Scotty stops dead in his tracks going up the stairs to the wheelhouse, but he doesn't look out to sea along with Comanche and me. He just holds his head even lower before continuing his walk up to the wheelhouse.

In a freakish occurrence, a scream in the fog is heard. A painful yell. The same agonizing scream the skipper gave while drifting away from the ship. The yell of a lost and broken man that met his demise.

But the gunshot happened before the scream?

Did he try to shoot at one of the sharks?

Did he commit to trying to shoot himself?

He couldn't possibly be alive out there.

What was he shooting at with one round, if not himself or the sharks?

Scotty continues on with his walk up to the wheelhouse, and never looks back out to sea. Comanche and I just watch the fog as the engines rev up and the ship starts to move away faster. I want to hope the morning sun is trying to push through the overcast. But the blackness of the storm in the other direction has now intermingled with the freezing fog.

We see a glow coming from the fog that is a deeper orange than the sun has to offer. And that strange orange glow is coming from the same general direction the skipper's life raft wandered into. It will take the best of seamanship to keep this boat out of the fog and away from the storm at the same time. And now, to add to the dread, we'll have to outmaneuver a strange orange glow following us in the fog.

"I've never seen an orange glow like that in fog. Do you think that's the sun trying to come through, maybe?" I ask Comanche, in hopes that he can answer with anything to cure my now constant sense of gloom.

But Comanche just grunts, shaking his head no.

"What the hell's out there, Comanche?" I ask.

"Sedna sends her demons for us..."

"I don't know if I want to know what that means," I say, while looking down.

Then he says the opposite of my hopes in calming my nerves.

"Soon... Very Soon..."

Chapter 17 - The Damned

Scotty quietly steers the ship. Our heading, northwest towards Canada. In calm seas, the journey may last a day or two. Scotty reminds us that we are relying on old sea navigation efforts, since all electronics are still fried from the lightning storm that happened, what feels like a week ago now. To the right of the ship, a freezing, gloomy, and blinding fog closes in the distance with that same orange glow that is following us. To our left, a hurricane type storm with clouds and waves that seem to be made of only the blackest heart and soul the sea can offer. Our tiny clear path of tame and frigid waters for the ship seems to close in by the hour with every mile we go. All is quiet. All are tense. Nothing can shake this sense of never-ending ruin, no matter how busy we try to stay.

Our hope is to flag down any vessel we see to get Diesel outta here faster. Radio in for more help to guide us into the nearest port. Any sign of human existence or civilization is what we all want. But this time of the year, this late in the season, the North Atlantic remains a desolate vast of cold, deadly blue water all hours of the day and night. Comanche and I clean up the deck from the earlier commotion with the skipper. I get a pair of binoculars and post up above the wheelhouse to embrace the cold air. With several layers to stay warm and my wetsuit to keep me dry, but nothing helps with braving the wind. Even my beanie hat feels frosted to my forehead. We take turns every thirty minutes. We keep the flairs we pulled from the life raft on standby in our makeshift crow's nest on top of the wheelhouse. We steam at full throttle all day and see nothing. No land. No other ships. Not even an airplane passing by in the sky. Not that we could see one that high in the air with the overcast that has loomed over us almost the entire journey now.

The oddest thing, though, if I had to narrow it down to one miniscule thing anyway, in looking through the binoculars, is how the fog and the storm seem to be closing in behind us. Like a clash of the mystic unknown to one side, and furious hatred of a storm on the other. At least that connection between the two is behind us and not ahead of us. But that blend seems to be closing in the gap with the ship faster and faster. Not to mention the orange glow that trails behind us in the fog. I have some suspicion that it may be the same ship of drug mules that attacked the speedboat or the same that granted the demise of the skipper. Possibly even the same ship that sent a mortar, or a single shot of cannon fire at the wheelhouse that killed Iceman. But why so elusive? Why remain following us in the fog? Why not make itself known and bring this ship down? The money that remains onboard is the only reason I can think of why it hasn't taken another shot at us.

Then there's also the suspicion that it may be something else. Something more sinister that I can't comprehend. Something not among the living. The lightning storm, the sharks, the whispering widow, this Sedna that Comanche speaks of, the dark voices and violins on a dead radio, a skipper that lost all touch with reality listening to them, and the coincidence of a storm system and fog that defies normalcy of maritime weather patterns. This gloomy view and all these thoughts are my only company sitting on top of this wheelhouse searching around for any glimpse of hope in any direction. I halt my trance of looking through binoculars and listening to my worries when I hear the engines rev down to a low RPM again. I look around on the deck and see Comanche coming up from below. He quickly marches up to the wheelhouse, and I make my way down from the crow's nest. I can hear Scotty talking to him, before I make my way inside.

"What's happening? Why'd we stop?" I ask.

"Diesel," Comanche says in a down voice.

"Good, you came down, Isaac. Let's go check on him. Ship's at idle and it'll stay in place. Let's go mates."

Scotty handles a few more controls behind the wheel to make sure the ship remains stationary against the currents. We all follow him down, but I jump ahead as soon as we get to the bunk room. Diesel is coughing blood and bile hard, to the point he can't take in a full breath. His eyes seem more yellow and his bandaged-up hand is covered in more blood. I can't tell if his hand started bleeding again or if it was the blood he was coughing out.

"Comanche, how long has he been coughing like this?" I ask, kneeling down beside the bunk.

I check his forehead and feel it is sweatier than ever. He flinches away at the touch of my icy hand, but at least his coughing slows down. I look up at Comanche and he just looks confused, but doesn't know how to answer. How would he know? We've been keeping watch above the wheelhouse since we sent the skipper adrift and started moving the ship. He could have just heard him coughing and came down to check. That's why Scotty wanted me to come down with them. His breathing is more of a struggled wheezing than actually taking in a breath, and he tries to mumble something before the cough comes back. He resorts to just laying his head down.

"You gotta calm down for me, Diesel. Alright? I gotta look over these bandages and we're gonna get another round of meds for you." I turn to Scotty, "Most of the left-over bandages and gauze are in here. But I need ibuprofen and anything to help keep this cough down. The one bite on his torso could have fractured some ribs if not broken them. So, we gotta get this cough calmed down or he could pierce a lung."

Diesel just grabs my arm and says in a struggling voice, "No…"

"We're just looking, Diesel. And we gotta change them out for some fresh bandages," I tell him.

"No!!!" He thrust my arm away from him. His frustration stuns me. I look back at Scotty and Comanche standing over me from behind, not knowing how to take it either.

"I'm done for, boys," he says, as he lays his head back down after another coughing spree.

I reach up and wipe the blood from his mouth. "At least let me look, Diesel… I just wanna look. Ok?"

"Go ahead," he says with his scratchy voice.

Even lifting the blankets off his legs may be painful for him, so I do it slowly. Both are black and blue with very little blood flow. His toenails have even turned gangrene. The infection must have traveled up to his lungs. The smell has gotten worse. The inner thigh wound has bled through all the bandages, only the blood is a brown, gray, and green mixture. I touch his feet and he doesn't even flinch. I look back up at Scotty, holding his hand over his nose and mouth to keep his composure.

"We're really close, Diesel... Right, guys?" I ask the two behind me. Comanche just shakes his head to agree. "You gotta hold out for us a day or so at the most."

"It's no use. I can't feel anything. They gonna take my legs."

"No, they're not. There's still plenty of blood flow going down there. You just gotta hang in there so we..."

He lifts his bandaged hand up to interrupt me. He just shakes his head no. "It's alright. I knew the sea would take me some day. I'm letting her have me on my terms. I want you to let her have me..." He coughs harshly again. "Scotty, Comanche... Be sure when I get wrapped up, there's enough weight on me so the sharks don't get me again. The cold shock will probably get me first. Don't be puttin' me in no damn freezer."

"Ok, Diesel. If that's what you want," Scotty tells him.

"No... We're not doing this again," I tell him. I turn to Comanche and Scotty, "We're not doing this again!"

"It's alright Isaac. It's alright… I need you to do something else for me. Comanche, can you pull my wallet out from those ripped up clothes? I think it's still in there." He lays his head back down and shivers again.

Comanche finds his blood-soaked wallet and hands it over to him. Diesel grabs it with his one good hand and lays it open on the blanket on top of his chest. Scotty drops on the bunk next to us, just looking down at the floor and shaking his head. Diesel fumbles through his overfilled wallet full of bank and business cards until he pulls out a neatly folded letter sealed in plastic wrap, folded down to only be about half the size of another business card. He brushes his wallet and everything he pulled out to the side of his chest. With his good hand, he reaches over to me and puts the folded letter in my palms while gripping my hand.

"Isaac… I need you to give this to my Boo. This is gonna be hard on her and my boys. Don't let the sea take you too. Don't be readin' it now. Just give it to her and she'll understand everything… Ok?"

"You're gonna give it to her yourself, Diesel. We're just a day away. You gotta hang in there for her."

He lets go of my hand and I look at the tiny plastic wrapped letter. Blood smears all over the outside of it. "It's not your choice, Isaac… It's mine…" He coughs again, dropping his good hand back down to his side.

The only thing that comes to mind holding this letter is the sinking feeling that even if I had a similar letter, I would have nobody to give it to. Nobody I knew knows that I'm here. There's nobody waiting for me to return. In a pathetic effort for a sense of relief in my own shattered heart, I turn to ask him, "I won't do it... I won't do it without knowing your real name first."

"What?" he asks.

"Your name. What's your real name?"

He smiles and scoffs before answering. "It's Phillip."

"What?" I turn to look at Scotty and Comanche and they are just as stunned as I am.

"Yeah... Phillip," he says again.

"Doesn't that mean like horse lover or somethin' like that, mates?" asks Scotty sarcastically to bring in some timely comic relief.

Diesel, or Phillip, starts to chuckle and struggles with the fluid in his lungs, but at least he's smiling. "Oh damn, boys... Don't make me laugh," he pleads while still laughing.

Scotty and I join in the laughter until Comanche adds in his two cents that tops Scotty's joke.

"Horse cock... Maybe? Yes?" Comanche says and we laugh harder.

Diesel points at Comanche, "Oh yeah... I'll take that one, you big ugly ox."

We all laugh with him, and I slip the letter into my pocket. "Dude, Diesel... You're like... Ya know... Black?"

"So ya noticed there, Greenhorn," Diesel says as the laughter from him, Comanche, and Scotty starts to fade off.

I give him one better than Comanche and Scotty combined, "But dude, Diesel... Phillip is like the whitest, white guy name ever man?" I tell him with obvious sarcasm. He just stops laughing suddenly and keeps a straight face.

"I know," he says. But he can't hold a straight face anymore. He burst into laughter so hard he tears up. We all laugh to the point of losing breath. I look back at Comanche and never knew he could laugh so hard. Even Scotty is rolling around in laughter on the bunk he sits on. I don't think we have all laughed this hard since the trip began. The last time I laughed this hard was... I can't remember any of my time in the Navy when I laughed this hard. The best part is that none of us are even drunk this time. Our laughter feels endless. The worst of all scenarios on the open ocean, everything that has gone wrong, and we all still laugh at giving each other crap, just for the fun of it.

Diesel keeps smiling and looking in our direction. His laughter subsides, but he keeps smiling. All of us keep laughing with him. At least I think we're laughing with him. He only stares back with blank eyes, but still smiling. I hold my hand up to quiet the other two's laughter behind me.

"Diesel?" I shake his shoulder. He just looks in our direction with a smile. Not a menacing smile, just a genuine smile from ear to ear, before it turns into just a mere grin. No movement from him and his arms lay lifeless at his side. No foul smoker's breath exiting his lips. I touch his neck to check for a pulse and feel nothing. For all the life he had in his veins has left him. It quietly left him with a smile. I turn back to Comanche and Scotty, still keeping my hand on Diesel's neck to feel for a pulse, but I just shake my head no.

"He's gone," Scotty says.

I don't know if Scotty is asking or just saying that. We all stare at Diesel's lifeless body on the bunk, trying to let it sink in. Now a second, even deeper sense of jealousy comes over me.

He had someone waiting for him back home to give a letter to.

And he left this world with a smile surrounded by his friends.

Comanche reaches over and closes Diesel's eyes.

Scotty puts a hand on my shoulder from behind me. "You did the best ya could, lad. I want ya to head on up and keep watch on deck for any passing vessels.

You know what he needed you to do for him. Now me and Comanche gotta do what we needed to do for him. We'll be up shortly, aye?"

I look down and try to take a breath, "Yeah…"

I look over at Comanche.

Then I get up and walk away. Nothing seems real anymore. I want this all to be a dream, but I know it isn't. It feels like the longest walk I have ever taken, making my way up to the wheelhouse. I grab the binoculars we left here, and the engine controls are just as they were when we went below. I climb up the ladder that takes me to the roof of the wheelhouse and everything feels numb to me. The cold air doesn't even phase me.

To one side the fog, the other is the storm, and our narrow corridor of hope is closing in on us all.

I have no tears to give Diesel, but I want to give them to myself somehow for not having anybody like he does.

I am truly lost.

Lost in a trance of looking out into the vastness of my first true love.

I am alone on top of the wheelhouse.

I am alone in this world now.

And this ship is all alone in this sea of the damned.

Because we are the damned and forgotten out here now.

Chapter 18 - Make Chase

A couple of hours later, on top of the wheelhouse alone with no other boats in sight, then Comanche and Scotty bring finally him up to the deck. Diesel's remains appear wrapped tightly in plastic wrap, tape, and a single heavy chain they must have found somewhere below deck. I make my way down to them as they set his body near the edge of the trawl door at the rear of the ship. Comanche goes back below deck and Scotty attaches one of the spare mini anchors from the dinghy boat to the chains wrapped around Diesel. He goes back to the winch controls and opens the trawl door.

I watch the body on deck, as if it's about to return to the land of the living, or maybe it's a matter of still trying to wake up from my dark nightmare. How many more will die out here before we make it back? How many more can the sea take before just making claim to the entire ship? The thought of just braving the storm so the dark abyss can put us out of our misery crosses my mind, but there would be no glorious end. There would be no epic battles, and nobody would know our story or struggles before the end. All we would learn to know is that it ends with only a hopeful last breath taken before water fills our lungs while all goes dark and quiet.

"He got it the best of us, aye lad?" Scotty says while looking down at the wrapped-up corpse near the edge of the deck.

"What?"

"Diesel… He left this life on his terms. He got it the best of us."

"Right," as I light up a smoke.

"Would you like to say a few words before we commit him to the sea like he wanted?"

"Why can't we just take him home and let his family bury him? We wrapped up Iceman and Dick and put them in the freezer. Why can't we just do the same thing?" I ask.

"Because it's the way he wanted it, Isaac… It's the way of the sea and he lived his life by it. We go home, back to shore, see our families, eat a decent meal, and make some babies. Then all we want to do after is to make it back out here to the sea. We live by it. We die by it. Either way, when she calls us, we answer her. I know a lot's happened since you been with us, but you've done well out here, lad. She called for you and you came. You look at young Diesel here and remember that there be worse ways to live and there's much worse ways to die. That's why you came, and I have no doubt when this is over, you'll keep coming back to her. Won't ya?"

I don't know how to answer him. I just shake my head yes, so he knows I heard everything he just said.

"I don't know where Comanche went, but he's not much for speaking anyways. I don't have no thoughtful words like a preacher man."

"I got the fisherman's prayer on the back of my St. Peter?"

"That would be good then, laddy…"

I reach for it and can't find it. I fidget around under my sweater and realize it's gone.

"What wrong?" Scotty asks.

"I just remembered I lost it. It got yanked off when I was helping Diesel on the boat after he was attacked." Scotty just looks down and bites his lip. "I can't remember the prayer off the top of my head, either." My heart sinks even lower into my stomach.

"It's alright, Isaac… I'm sure it was a nice prayer, aye?"

Comanche came back up from below at some point. He taps me on the back of my shoulder. I turn around and see him holding my violin case, then lifts it up to hand it to me.

He tells me, "Sad song…"

Such a gray day surrounded by a turmoil of events and death. This sad attempt at a funeral would be fitting for most of the tunes I know how to string from memory, but I just shake my head no.

He holds the violin case closer to me, hoping I'll take it and says, "Please…"

I take the case from him and he walks over to Diesel's body next to Scotty. I walk forward towards the edge of the trawl door. I find a spot to sit so the slowly rocking boat doesn't throw off my balance. I stroke a tune to adjust my bow. The only tune I know by heart comes to mind. The only type of tune that makes sense right now. I look out to the sea behind us and my soul leaves me in knowing the connecting fog and storm have combined and is now closing the distance to the ship. Comanche says something in a low voice, maybe even chanting something, while leaning over Diesel's body, but I can't understand whatever language he speaks in. *Wayfaring Stranger* comes across the strings with little effort for me. Probably the best way I have managed to play this violin in years, and it came at the most needed of times for our newly departed ship mate. Maybe I play it so well for all of them we've lost. Maybe I play it so well right now for all of us, living or not.

Scotty tosses the small anchor out the back of the boat. The chains around Diesel's corpse tighten from the weight and they guide his remains off the back of the ship. They walk beside him until the water takes him. He doesn't float for very long and his body disappears from our sight to drop down into the ocean. To leave this world and be committed to the depths of the deep blue beyond. I'm sure he will sink fast as he requested before his last breath. I don't know what's beyond death. I honestly never try to think about it much. But the last few days of being surrounded by it, I wouldn't want to know that my remains became a fresh meal for the sharks that trail his sinking body. That is, if I was aware as to the results of my physical remains at that point.

A burst of cold air removes me from my musical trance. Not just cold air but freezing air from the fog that has closed in on us during our attempt at a funeral. Scotty and Comanche have already made their way towards the control panel to close the trawl door. Then I hear it. I hear a sound that I thought couldn't be heard again. The radio was tossed over before we sent the skipper adrift. That sound of a screeching out of tune violin echoes from out of the patchy frozen fog attempting to overcome the ship. It plays with a few strokes of a scratchy bow. No particular tune, just an effort to make noise with the strings on a violin. I stand up and look out beyond the trawl door, leaving the violin and bow at my side. It can't be coming from the fog, but it is louder than my violin tune that I was just playing.

"Best be gettin' a bit more practice there on that tune, Isaac," jokes Scotty as he keeps walking away.

I turn back and see the front of the ship, but they don't notice that the fog and the storm in front of us have also collided together. They just talk with each other, not paying attention, that it isn't me playing a scratchy violin tune. I don't know what to say or think. The mixture of storm clouds and freezing fog is in front of us and behind us. Scotty and Comanche finally look up to notice how black the skies have become. The scratchy violin from the distance plays louder and pierces our ears.

They both look back at me and I just hold my violin and bow up in the air to show them that it isn't me playing. In the confusion, we all look up at the dark clouds above us. The distant violin stops, and the low grumble of thunder takes its place. They both look at me with a level of concern that chills my spine more than the freezing fog already has. But they are not looking at me. They are looking at the orange glowing presence in the distance of the fog that is too patchy to make anything clear. But that orange glow is now moving faster than ever.

The fog opens up to reveal the thing that is haunting us, relentlessly tormenting us from a realm incomprehensible for any living man. Because it is comprised of such an evil, it can only be ferried by the dead. This orange glow was the culprit to this constant surrounding doom all along. In the distant frozen and patchy fog, a ship sails with all three of its masts a blaze. A fire with flames so high and burning hot, it clears a path through the fog as it approaches.

Whether it be a schooner or frigate, I do not recall my naval history well enough to tell. But what is for certain is that it slowly looms out of the fog and makes its presence known to the three of us to place a feeling of emanate demise in our already broken hearts and souls. It comes with sails of fury and flames under the blackness of evil and stormy skies. Every inch of it burns brightly. Beings, whether or not human, scurry around onboard a smoldering deck to adjust the scorching sails. We remain frozen in fear, a fear deeper than what has tried to overtake us thus far. Fear and dread of the ship that comes to collect the corrupt. A ship with hulls made of brimstone. A ship that comes with sails of a never-ending fire.

"Man of War," Comanche says in a terrified voice.

Scotty's look of fear matches my own. "Come Isaac. Get away from the trawl door so I can close it."

I look back again to hear the broken violin tune playing again in the distance this time. The burning ship is nearly half a mile away from us as it makes its turn towards us. How those burning sails aid in steering the ship in any way is a feat of the paranormal. I walk away from the trawl door as Scotty closes it. Comanche is already above near the wheelhouse with a pair of binoculars in hand. Scotty and I run up to join him. None of us can believe our eyes. None of us can explain this malicious apparition gliding above dark waters behind us as if it's unharmed by its own flames.

Scotty uses the second pair of binoculars to look for himself. "Good God help us…"

Comanche hands me his pair and I see the thing that has placed a level of terror into us that would instantly kill the weak-hearted. Everyone, or thing, on board is engulfed in flames and still moving about unscathed by the flames that consume them. Tightening lines, stowing ropes, and moving cannons. Actual cannons. Each charred and simmering skeletal figure struggles to move the cannons like a living person would. A dark black figure of a man, smoking from the fire, but not engulfed like the rest of the crew, stands at the wheel slightly out of sight. But he remains perfectly still, staring at our ship with burning red eyes underneath a large rounded hat. Above him is the worst of all. Hanging in the various lines crossing the masts is a distinct figure in modern clothing. Clothing still seared and tarnished from the flames that engulf the ship, but modern rain and wet gear is what he wears.

Only, the person wearing the yellow rain gear is strung up by the neck in a noose. The body flinches and jerks around while being charred by the ship's flames. The yellow jacket quickly turns black and melts to the person who still struggles to hold on to any life left. But I know it's Yellow Jack being strangled. The moments that pass by make me believe Yellow Jack is already dead. This is just a tortured rendering of what's left of him, because his head turns all the way around to look at us on our lowly fishing vessel. His head completely turns backwards in the noose, but his body does not follow. His shoulder only turns enough to raise an arm pointing in our direction. His face seared and burned down to the bone in most places. Both of his lips gone to reveal a skeleton that has a permanent smile as he still jerks and flails around in the noose. Yellow Jack has joined a vessel of the wicked and the damned. Now he points at us through the flames of his own demise in the form of a fierce ghost ship.

"We have to go…"

"It can't be true, can it?" Scotty says.

A loud, deep thud is heard from the direction of the flaming ghost ship. I raise the binoculars again to see the scorching skeletal remains of sailors stand behind a cannon, laughing and pointing at us. Only the cannon has smoke coming from the end of the barrel.

"Shit!!!!" I rush towards Scotty and Comanche with all my weight to throw us all down to the surface of the walkway surrounding the wheelhouse. A cannon ball bounces around on the deck below, bashing right through the winch control panel, destroying everything in its path and lunges out the side of the ship. "YES!!! IT'S VERY FUCKING TRUE AND WE HAVE TO GO NOW!!!!!"

We rush to the wheelhouse and Scotty turns the engines on full power. That's the first time we get a solid view of the storm to the left and the fog to the right colliding as one in the path ahead. Our already narrow corridor of calm waters to travel through has turned to a hateful dark duo of sinister weather. I look out the back glass of the wheelhouse to see the burning ship has completed its turn at us, with cannons facing our ship as she makes chase. Another cannon fire goes off, but lands several feet behind us in the water.

"She whispers," Comanche says.

I turn around to see that Scotty holds the controls with a death grip, turning his knuckles white. Neither of them has contemplated the storm ahead of us. Scotty just put the ship in full throttle. No talk has been made between us in what feels like the last several minutes, because we see her at the front of the ship from the wheelhouse. We see the dark figured woman looking right at us from the front of the ship. The storm clouds have rushed us, or maybe our boat moves that fast into the storm to escape the burning ship. I do not know. Either way, the threatening clouds open up with lightning and rain. Rain and hail so hard that we can't hear anything. All we see is that damned whispering widow looking at us through the rain as her feet lift off the deck. All the thunder comes at once. Her dress flutters and flaps in the wind. Water from the high seas splashes the deck, but she doesn't move from her hovered stance. More lightning reflects across dark high seas that make the ship feel like the beginnings of a roller coaster.

But all goes quiet again before the coming thunder. Even the rain suddenly stops and the window frosts over, but we still see her. Raising higher and higher from the deck with her arms outstretched. She looks up at us from under her long hair and motions her hands across her neck, as if slicing her own throat with malice and hatred again. Then we all hear her whisper. A whisper that we wish we didn't hear or prefer it to be muffled out by the storm, but we heard her say it in a whisper.

"Burn in the bay…"

The thunder comes along with more lightning and she disappears before our eyes. We look all around the ship through the windows we can see through, but she's simply gone again. I grab the binoculars and look out the back window. I can't tell what is thunder and what is cannon fire from that burning ship. If it still shoots at us, we are just beyond its range as long as Scotty keeps the ship ahead. With a storm like this, that ship can glide with the heavy winds in any direction it wants with little effort. Yellow Jack just points and almost appears to be laughing at us as he still hangs in the swinging noose. But that other dark figure. The one with red eyes just looks back at me with an older style spyglass from behind the wheel of the ship. Our ship rocks and tilts around with each massive wave that feels like it's coming from all directions. I lose my footing and drop to the floor.

"Are we pushing into that storm?!" I get back up, bracing myself on one of the control panels next to Scotty.

Scotty just shakes his head in unease. "We're already in it, matey! I have the wheel, now! You and Comanche, batten down all hatches and seal off the hull! We gotta stay ahead of that phantom. Tighten down anything that isn't stowed away already! Get out there on deck now before this storms starts gettin' real pissy with us now, lads!!!"

Chapter 19 - A Storm of Fire

When freezing water isn't splashing us over the side of the ship, the hail coming down scratches our bare hands that hold on to any rails we can use to brace ourselves. The rocking ship travels up and down mountains of frigid water. Lightning strikes are our only visibility now to gauge the monstrous size of the waves that come in all directions. The tops of my hands, shoulders, and back of my neck take a pounding from the hail. Comanche slips around on the deck with every step as we both try to muscle everything into a secure spot. Every porthole has to be closed. Every loose item is locked down. The dinghy boat and life rafts are at the ready for the worst-case scenario. Every door has to be sealed shut. While Comanche and I are below deck, Scotty braves the storm from behind the wheel. I can hear cannon fire within the thunder. That thing, that wicked burning phantom ship, still shoots at us from the distance.

Comanche and I move as fast as we can. We have been on some rough seas since I've been out with these guys, but nothing like this. He points at anything that needs to be fastened down in some manner. Water has come inside the lower levels of the ship enough to cover our boots. This storm came in on us faster than expected, but none of us have time to think about how or why it came in so freakishly fast. None of us register that the fog to one side and the storm on the other is an evil force that demands our reckoning.

Comanche and I move to the engine room to turn on the pumps to force out any excess water that has flooded in. We both get tossed around with the roaring sea. I get thrown back down the stairs as we make our way up from the engine room. Comanche lifts me back up on my feet one-handed and we continue to the deck. The crane for winching the nets just flings around with each wave. Scotty tries to point it out with the spotlight. I can see him yelling and pointing at it from the wheelhouse. With each change in the ship's direction, the crane shifts all the weight around, almost toppling the ship over.

Comanche commits to braving the open deck as water and hail pounds down on us from every direction. With the noise of the water, the thunder, and the hail, we can't even hear each other yelling. I grab his arm before he walks out on the deck, holding the rail. I point to the ropes that have been stowed away in one of the gear boxes. I let a swell push me directly into it and I open it up to grab a section of rope Comanche and I can tie ourselves off with before walking out on the open deck. One rogue wave and it would send us flying overboard without a rope attached to the railing. Comanche shakes his head yes and we both tie ourselves off to the rail. He sees the steel cables dangling from the crane system above. We slowly make our way to it within arm's reach, then I let go of the rail to get a grip of the cable. The rope burns on my unhealed and shredded palms from pulling in Diesel after the shark attack, but I don't care. Not with a storm like this, muffling out my screams of pain. With a storm like this, everything becomes a matter of survival, even if only functioning on adrenaline.

I catch a glimpse of the burning ship behind us. It's visual burns into me with a terror that I have never felt before. Burning deep into me as its sight comes and goes behind the waves that trail us. It gained on us while we were below deck. I hold the steel cable while Comanche tries to tie it off, but the burning ship takes another shot at us.

"GET DOWN!!!" I scream at Comanche as I let the steel cable go. I lunge at him to fall on the deck and we feel our ship quake and tremble with a direct hit on the back side.

I look up at the wheelhouse and see Scotty raise up from his covered spot. I can see flashes and strobes going off from where he is inside the wheelhouse. He scrambles around with the controls. Comanche and I get up from the freezing wet deck, checking the ropes around our waist while still holding the rails.

Scotty points the light at us as he reaches for the loudspeaker microphone, *"That was a direct hit!! We're losing oil pressure in an engine and I got a fire alarm going off!! Get back down there and put it out! Leave the crane for now, I'll keep her steady from here, lads!! HURRY!!"*

Comanche ties off the crane cable with a temporary knot that we can only hope holds. We both untie our ropes and head back below into the engine room. I grab the fire extinguisher from the kitchen area and Comanche, busting through the wall mounted glass casing with his fists, grabs one from the corridor. We both shift around like ping-pong balls in the narrow corridor that leads to the engine room. Everything is a blur of sparking electricity and alarm strobes. The dizziness, the chaos, and the noise, all combined, makes it nearly impossible to accomplish anything. Once in the engine room, I spray the extinguishers on the light fixtures, so they stop sparking. The hull is bashed in, letting in some frigid water, but not fully compromised. Only, it has severely bent and sliced into the fuel and oil lines that lead to the one engine that has been knocked off its bolted mounting studs.

I hear another round of cannon fire from outside, but it muffles out with splashing sounds, indicating that it missed the ship. Comanche and I try to assess the damage, but we both know it's no use. We are one engine down. I move the water pump hose around at my feet to get more of the water out of here, but when I look down at the water raising above our feet, I bend over to roll my hands in it and lift them up. The water is laced with oil and fuel, so much it hardly rolls off my hands, even with all the water coming through.

I hit Comanche on the backside, and he turns to see me showing him my oil and fuel covered hands. Anything this water pump in the engine room sucks up right now, will be laced with fuel and boating oil leading out to sea from the exit hoses on the side of the ship. Comanche does a double take at my hand to see the oil. He turns around to one of the engine control panels to shut down the compromised engine. The fuel shut off for the engine is underneath the dislodged engine, with no way to stop the fuels from flowing out. He has me place the pump next to the smashed in portion of the hull to make sure the pumps take in as little fuel and oil as possible. But there's no stopping the flow of fuel and oil out of the engine room. With only one engine running, we'll leave a deadly trail of diesel and oil behind us until the fuel supply can be shut off or we run out.

Neither of us wants to be in here any longer than necessary. We head back up to the deck and keep a grip on the rails to the wheelhouse. The hail has stopped, but the waves and swells have gotten bigger. I cannot tell what is rain coming down and what is sea water splashing over the deck higher than the ship. The wheelhouse door swings open with the wind and Comanche helps me push myself inside. Scotty frantically steers the wheel and tries to manage all the controls. The alarms that are sounding pierce our eardrums. Everything that was loose in the wheelhouse rolls around on the floor. Coffee cups, wet paperwork blowing around from the winds, ash trays full of old cigars and cigarette buds, all flung about on the floor. In a fit of stress or anger, Comanche pulls out his massive bowie knife and stabs the smoke alarm, the sound whirring down to a struggled buzz before shutting off. He then calmly closes the door and drops to the floor to catch his breath.

"What's the damage?" Scotty asks.

"It looks like they got a direct hit at the hull near the rudder and bashed it in against the engine. It only broke through enough to knock off the motor mounts and start flooding the engine room. But there is something else…"

Comanche gets up and grabs the binoculars to look to the backside of the ship to check on how close the burning phantom is now.

Scotty just turns and looks down at me, still sitting on the floor, bracing myself against one of the counters in the wheelhouse. "Well, spit it out, aye!"

"We're down to one engine and the fuel and oil lines were damaged under the weight of the engine that broke off. The water pumps that are keeping the flooding under control are also pumping out a trail of oil and fuel behind us."

Scotty grumbles and spins the wheel as fast as he can to maneuver through the stormy seas ahead of us. "Bullocks!! That's just fuckin' bullocks!! Can't get any worse than this, mateys. We'll burn that single engine out trying to push through much more of this."

"It's worse," Comanche says, as he looks out the rear of the ship.

Scotty and I turn to look at him, his back is turned to us as he looks out the rear windows with the binoculars still. I stand up and he hands me the pair to see through for myself. And what I see is something that can only be described as yet another dreadful depiction of evil that even the darkest portions of man's imagination could never fathom. The phantom ship is right on our tail. All the burning and tortured souls on board stand at the ready, aiming a cluster of cannons at our ship, smiling and gnashing their teeth through melted skin. The blazing phantom vessel remains unscathed by the stormy seas. It is a fiery seafaring hearse for the masses that were at once the lost and the damned of the sea. Only, every part of the ocean surrounding the burning ship is also on fire now from our leaking fuel and oil. Yet, the phantom ship's blaze only glows brighter, the flames of the sails grow higher, and the crew more active in their duties to attend to the demise of the Sea Hellion as the phantom glides closer to us over the violent sea now made of fire.

The flames on the ocean that follow our trail are broken off by the multitude of swells and breaking waves. But that slight glimpse of hope in seeing our trail of fuel for the flame being broken is shattered. Glass and pieces of the boarded-up windows are sent flying throughout the wheelhouse while we were all looking at the burning phantom ship. The roar of the winds and violent sea come into the wheelhouse to break our trance in observing the doom that follows closely behind us. The crane and multiple steel cables fling about on and above the deck. Comanche's temporary knot with the steel cable has failed, and we both forgot to secure it better before returning to the wheelhouse.

"God dammit!!!"

Now we're all back down on the floor again, looking for any cover. My hands and knees shuffle through the broken glass to get back on my feet.

"Are we alright!?" Scotty yells out and looking at both of us closely. He helps Comanche back up on his feet before rushing to the wheel. Just to drop low again to avoid the crane that has swung away and now returning to crash against the wheelhouse again. Comanche wastes no time getting back down to the deck. Scotty still struggles with the wheel and maneuvering the ship against the swells and breaking waves.

"Get down there with him, Isaac! Don't let him go alone!"

I take another look out the back with the binoculars to see the burning ship still coming closer. But its crew is struggling in the effort to reload the older style cannons, mainly because everything is on fire. One of them is engulfed in more flames than it already had from attempting to load the gunpowder. The flinching and burning sailor just gets engulfed in flames and falls overboard into the water, while the others point and laugh at him.

"Isaac, GO NOW!!!" Scotty yells again.

With no time to spare as the phantom ship reloads, I run out of the wheelhouse to help Comanche tie down this damn crane again. At the bottom of the stairs, I tie myself off to the railing and grab the spare rope to have Comanche do the same. With the control panel to the winch and the crane destroyed, we either have to reel it in manually or tie the crane down to the ship in multiple locations. Comanche grabs a wrench and a pipe for some leverage to commit to reeling everything in by hand. He had already grabbed the end of the crane cable before I made my way down. I hold on to Comanche's belt and post up beside him and we turn the pulley in with all our strength. The ship tosses from side to side and throws me down to the other side of the deck as far as the rope around my waist will allow.

Comanche stays in place and keeps turning the pulley with all his might. The weight and resistance he turns right now with a single extended wrench is insane, but every muscle he has is needed now more than ever. I slip around the deck, trying to get my footing back to make my way over to him. Comanche has already reeled in the crane, almost to the point where it can be locked in place and secured. He grunts and growls, veins swell from his tattooed forehead, blood burst through his hands from his epic grip. He yells out in pain louder and louder with each turn, but somehow keeps his footing and locks the pulley in place before I even get back to him. He loosens up his grip, gasping for air once he feels the crane has been reset.

"Yeah!!! Hell yeah, Comanche!!! You did it," I tell him, while spitting out some of the salt water that had splashed on deck and in my face. I just wave my free arm around with a thumbs up and smile as we celebrate a small victory. He drops down to slump on top of the pulley that just took all his energy and strength. He doesn't smile much, and the stormy sea is roaring so loud that we can hardly hear each other celebrate what most would assume is a minute win. But he looks up at me with a smile and gives me a thumbs up in return while still catching his breath.

"FREAK WAVE!!! Freak wave, starboard side!!! Freak wave, starboard side!!! Hold tight, gents," Scotty yells at us through the intercom.

The spotlight is pointed to the right of the ship and my heart sinks in, realizing the monster wave is too close to make a run back to the wheelhouse. The ship turns sideways as the wave approaches and we are almost completely on our side. I hold the rail tight, hugging it with both arms and Comanche does the same near the crane control. Scotty panics to turn the front of the ship away from the wave, but the Sea Hellion is already tipped over too far. My feet dangle freely, pointing down at the water. The wave breaks, sending thousands of gallons of the sea crashing down on us as Scotty tries to turn the boat away. My grip slips under the force of the wave and my back feels like it almost breaks when my attached rope tightens up as I'm thrusted into the frigged waters.

The ship turns away from the breaking wave before any more water washes over the deck. We ride the wave down and I hold onto my rope with all the strength I can manage from my hands that have taken too much abuse.

"ISAAC!!!"

Comanche has been tossed overboard and is being swept away into the storm. I hold the rope with one arm, trying to keep my head above water and reach for him. The fear in his face is soul crushing. The trembling of both our hands from the freezing water allows neither of us to keep a good grip on the other. He slips right through my numb and slashed up hands as more of the breaking wave comes from the back side of the ship now.

"COMANCHE!!!"

He swims in a panic, but the last of the breaking wave and the vast amounts of gear that have been broken away from the deck, slams on top of him, pushing him under the sea. He struggles with the netting and buoys. The wave and the winds take him further away from the ship. The lightning only gives me a glimpse of the gear that commits to sinking, but I don't see him struggling anywhere. My screams of hatred for the storm of such fierce biblical power are muffled out by the following thunder and the waters that still crash down all around me with growing intensity. The ship returns to a steadier position as I struggle to pull myself back up on the deck. Comanche's rope that I forgot to tie him off with still flaps next to the pulley for the crane that he muscled in place on his own. At the bottom of the wheelhouse, I toss my rope aside and slowly head up to Scotty. Head down and distraught for yet another friend that the ocean has taken from me, with no guilt or hesitancy on the sea's part. She, the sea, truly covets all of us to the point of no return. The sea has claimed him. The sea will not stop until it claims all of us. Whether it be this epic storm toppling over our broken vessel or the burning ship shooting us down to hell in a frenzy of cannon fire, the sea will have us before this night ends.

"Where's Comanche?!" Scotty yells, still behind the wheel that he steers frantically.

"I had him in my hands… He was right there!!!"

"What?"

I drop to the floor with my head in my torn-up hands. My blood is all over my hands. I don't know if it's blood or saltwater all over my face.

"Comanche's blood all over my hands. Diesel and Iceman are all over my hands!!!"

He locks the wheel in place and turns around. He shakes and jolts me by the shoulders to knock me out of my state of despair. "Where's Comanche, damn you!?!?"

"He was swept away… The freak wave got him and swept him away. I had him in my fucking hand!"

Scotty just looks down at me. Tears fill his eyes before he turns around to unlock the wheel and keep steering us through the storm. That's when I see the duffle bag at his feet, tucked away under the steering control dash. The same type of duffle that Yellow Jack came on the ship with. The same type of duffle filled with drugs and then exchanged for Canadian dollars. All the windows and boards for the front of the wheelhouse have been smashed in already. Water floods and splashes in with every wave Scotty tries to maneuver through. I get up and look out the back window that isn't broken. The burning phantom ship is gone from view. I wait for a few seconds to see if it has just lost distance between us and is hidden in the waves, but it isn't anywhere behind us.

"Good God in heaven," Scotty mumbles under his breath. His eyes are white and mouth wide open with the quivering lips of a terrified child. Not a single concern for the treacherous seas ahead of us as he looks out the broken window to the side of our ship. Coming down a large swell like a gliding chariot of the apocalypse, the burning phantom ship has bested us in treading through the damning storm. It comes with a deadly speed and high flames. All the flaming figures on board are pointing at us, snarling at us, and laughing at us as they smolder in their own bodies, devoured in a hell fire on the deck of brimstone. I can hear them all screaming and crying out. I can hear them mocking and ridiculing us for our miniscule attempts to escape our own doom that we have created. I can hear them through the storm and raging winds above the waters. I can hear them growling and ready to feast on our departed souls when this body ends.

Only the darkest and heinous of dead men on that ship stands quietly behind the wheel under that large round hat. But his eyes are more red and fiercer than the rest. One arm remains at the wheel, the other has a sabre in hand. The captain of the phantom has placed his ship right next to ours. All their guns, pistols, rifles, and cannons are at the ready, aimed directly at our hull. The Jolly Rodger, tattered and torn, waves high above the ship's flames. He points his sabre at us with a gruesome and dreadful scream. Serving as the cue his demon sailors needed to unleash a raging wrath of lethal cannon inferno down on us. No words, nor screams can come from within me or could even be heard if I tried while the skies open up on us. Only now to send down a true storm of fire and absolute madness.

Chapter 20 - Abandon Ship

Hell comes down on us all at once. The gun fire, the storm, the shattering and twisting steel through the deck of the ship and its shrapnel is sent in all directions. Explosions are above and below deck in a frenzy of blasts and bullets. Scotty and I can't even hear each other yelling in the wheelhouse as the phantom ship sends all its ferocity of cannon fire at us. The lights go out all around to leave us cowering low inside the darkness of the wheelhouse. The dissipating lightning storm and the flames from the phantom ship are the only light we have to see in front of us. The Sea Hellion has tipped over to its side from the cannon fire and taking on water. The sea, still daunting at our sinking ship, thrust us around even harder now that all engines and power has been lost. The side window of the wheelhouse is now underwater. The black depths of the ocean are at my feet as I look down. Scotty struggles with the money filled duffle bag under the ship's wheel and he resorts to stuffing the Canadian bills into his jacket.

"Leave it, Scotty! Just leave it!!!" I yell, as I grab him by the shirt and pull him up as the water pours in. He commits to cramming more in his jacket in a panic. I push up the side window of the wheelhouse that is still above water, but for how long I don't know. The phantom ship has docked right next to us, and the crew, still in the flames, are throwing over ropes to keep the Sea Hellion from sinking any more than it already has. Even worse, they are using those same ropes to board our ship.

Their flaming bodies, multitudes of them, with knives in their mouths and swords attached to their backs, hang upside down on the rope to crawl across them. All this, while their ship and all of them are still on fire. Only, the further away they get from their own flaming ship, the less vigorous their own individual flames are. They move like a horde of demons. They burn like monsters trying to escape Satan's grasp, but when their flames go out to a mere smoldering char of human flesh, they resemble a band of living dead pirates. They stand on the deck next to random flames from the fuel still escaping our ship, and they walk on the deck as if the ship were not even laying on its side.

"We have to go! They're coming, Scotty!!"

I keep reaching for him so we can make our escape out the side window, still above water. I look to the back side of the ship and the small dinghy boat floats upside down on top of the water in the distance on a rope still attached to the ship. I look forward and through the lightning and see one of the dead pirates has a classic pistol pointed at the wheelhouse. It just stands there and smiles, with its rotting and scorched black face. Many of them smile, as if they were never on fire, and they growl and snarl like rabid dogs toying with its prey. A horde of a dozen of them can be seen through the flames of their burning ship behind them.

The one with the gun has them all hold in place and it looks right at me, still pointing that flint style pistol. He points it down at a cable system and grimly laughs and the other's laugh with him. The cable he points the pistol at is the crane and winch system. One shot will send the entire crane at the wheelhouse again and that thing, that dead smoldering pirate thing, just looks and laughs with the gun pointing at it. It just stands there with its pistol at the ready, despite the flames coming up at it from below deck. I drop back down into the flooding wheelhouse to find cover.

"I got all I can carry! Here, take some of this, lad!" Scotty yells.

BANG!!!

A single gunshot goes off and I can hear the steel cables of the crane system unraveling.

"Scotty, get away from the wheel!!!"

The crane crashes in the front of the wheelhouse before either of us can register what happened. Scotty goes under the water that fills up half the wheelhouse on its side. I drop below the freezing water and reach for anything, hoping the crash of the crane didn't kill him. He grabs my hand before I can find him but holds me down with all his weight. I manage to get his head above water, and he screams in pain with his first gasp of air. I hold us both above water with the captain's chair that is mounted to the floor.

"My leg! My leg is caught and broken, Isaac," he yells over the raging storm outside.

"I got ya. I got ya. Just keep your head above water. Hold this chair and I'll go down and look..." I take a deep breath and follow his torso and leg down. The crane system has lodged him against the side of the wheelhouse. I can feel his leg is mangled in multiple places underneath it. I come back up for air and the wheelhouse has filled in with more water. The Canadian currency he had stuffed in his jacket floats all around inside the flooding room. I just hold him up above water and look right back at him while my lips shiver from the cold water. Neither of us have any words of comfort for the other. There is no possible way to get him dislodged from underneath that crane.

"Scotty," but no words can leave my mouth for a moment. "I'm not gonna go on living through this one by myself, old man."

A sad attempt at ignoring our nearing demise. He pauses for a bit, spitting out the water that still fills the room up to his chin now.

"Yes you are lad... Yes you are."

"No... Scotty." We both struggle to stay above water now.

"She calls for me, Isaac," panting for air in pain. "You just go on now, boy. She calls for me. Don't let her take you too... You live." I look down at him and hesitate. I don't know what to do. I don't know what to think or say. I can't leave him. We both hear footsteps coming closer. Footsteps from the demon pirates growling along with the thunder outside the wheelhouse. His head is almost under water now, spitting out the sea in his final moments. Until he lunges up at me, just to yell, "GO NOW, BOY!!!"

I rush to the window of the wheelhouse above the water. As soon as my torso is up, a ghost pirate that was about to make its way in screams at me as its scorching face remains covered in fire. It looks up at me while growling and snarling. It raises up a sword for a hand as it goes to swing it at my head. As it lunges back, I hear several knuckles get crushed from punching its exposed boney jaw as hard as I can. A cluster of teeth, one of them golden, are slung into the water as it loses grip and falls backward from the blow of my right hook. I look down at Scotty once more as I scramble out the window. His head is now below water, but his hands jerk and flail around from drowning. More pirates are scrambling to get up to the wheelhouse. They snarl and growl at every movement, as if none of them can actually speak, just grinding teeth and grunting commands at each other.

I jump down into the freezing water behind the wheelhouse that is sinking fast. I stay close to the rails of the ship still above water and follow them to the back of the ship. The other demons, crawling and walking around like spiders, either don't know I'm not in the wheelhouse anymore or never knew I was there. I look back as I stay low in an attempt not to make a splash while moving along the railing. Every inch of their bodies is either burned or rotted to the bone. Two of them drop down into the wheelhouse and I hear Scotty screaming. They have pulled him up in time before he committed to drowning. His legs are mangled up from the force of them, jerking him out from under the water and crane as if he was weightless to their abnormal level of strength for soulless rotting corpses.

Scotty still screams and jerks around as one holds him up by the torso and chews on his upper shoulder near his neck. More join in the feast on Scotty, but they only bite and laugh with each chunk of his flesh that they spit out. Not enough to kill him off, but to maim him further in his final moments. Another pirate pulls out a sabre to thrust into his stomach while they still hold him up in the air. The sword goes right through him and out his back, making more pirates laugh and snarl. They tie his hands behind his back with a rope. All Scotty can do is gasp as he looks down at the sword through his stomach. A noose that was tied to their ship came with one of the dead pirates and is tossed around Scotty's neck. The lead pirate that was holding Scotty up while they put the rope around his neck, drops him down into the water.

Other clusters of demon pirates, still engulfed in flames while on the phantom ship, heave at the rope they attached Scotty to. They pull with the strength of an entire living crew, dozens of them, rotting and burning. Scotty is hoisted up by his neck, a sword still in his gut and life still in his limbs twitching around. He is hung high beside the remains of Yellow Jack near the burning sails of the phantom ship. The one demon behind the wheel of the phantom ship, the one that stands tall and firm with the large hat and burning red eyes, continues to look in my direction with those eyes made of a bright red fury. None of the other demon pirates are looking for me. Just gloating and shooting their flint pistols into the air and clanging swords together in a sickening celebration of yet another soul claimed by them in stormy seas.

I continue to quietly slither my way down the back side of the ship, but I hear a different growl. I turn back again and it's the same one that I knocked teeth out of, snorting and grunting at the rest while pointing in my direction. With no more effort in sneaking around in the water, I move fast towards the rope holding the small boat, bouncing around upside down in the choppy waters behind the ship. I grab the rope to bring it in closer, but the winds and the currents are too strong.

So now, I'm completely in the water with the sinking ship behind me. Another look in the corner of my eye and the horde of evil dead pirates is slowly walking towards the end of the ship. They walk along the sinking ship as if the storm and the winds hold no bearing against them. Only the flames they are lightly shrouded in give off the hint that the winds of the storm are still upon us. The toothless pirate, with a sword for an arm, is moving faster than the rest. A burning rage and taste for revenge gives him the means to move towards me faster than the others. But they are all still on top of the sinking Sea Hellion, while I am several feet into the open ocean holding onto the rope that can lead me to my only source of a life raft in the form of a motorless dinghy boat.

I take in a lung full of freezing saltwater as I am pulled under into the darkness. I look up above me in a panicky swim, and all I see is the outline of my life raft from the orange glow of the burning ship. The pain passes up my leg and into my spine as I scream underwater. I look down to see a shark with its eyes rolled back and trying to take a continued chop at my calf muscle. The amount of teeth and vast strength is overwhelming as I go down further and further.

It bites again at my foot and my face is right next to its eyes and gills as it tries to swim down even further. The only thing I have is a small fillet knife in my belt and I try to pull it out while this thing thrusts me around several feet under water. I pull it out and take several jabs at its gill slits. I hit it with a rapid fire of knife jabs until it has both my blood and its own blood flooding into my nostrils and mouth and it finally lets its jaw loose. I nearly lose my knife on the swim back to the surface but maintain a grip on it. I catch the epic size of the white shark that tried to take my leg. It swims above and around in a frenzy, filling the water with blood from its fresh wounds on its gills. Or maybe that's my blood. Other smaller sharks begin to close in.

"FUCK!!!!" I come up to the surface, screaming in pain. The current leads me right back to the rope that is attached to the boat. The demonic burning pirates are right at the sinking ship's edge. I pull myself up onto the upside-down boat and yell out in more pain than I have ever felt before. The toothless pirate has jumped into the water and is committed to ending me. It pulls himself along the same rope with its one good hand and wades that sword hand in the water. I cut the rope to the boat, but it keeps swimming after me with absolute rage and sends out a demonic growl that can be heard over the thunderous sea and the sounds of the sinking Sea Hellion. It swims with all its ferocity and I ready my tiny fillet knife to get a good stab at it before it can puncture and sink my dinghy raft. I drift away from the sinking ship with the burning phantom on the other side of it, but I don't drift away with the current fast enough. This living corpse of a pirate keeps swimming after me, growling and snarling with missing teeth in its jaw made of visibly burned up bone and flesh.

Without warning, the pirate is rapidly thrusted around just a few away feet from puncturing my boat. It grunts in panic and I can see tail and dorsal fins surrounding it. My attacker has made the fatal bite towards something that is already dead. The pirate is pulled under water and then brought back up again. The only difference here is that the demon pirate laughs. It laughs as it still tries to come towards me with no regard for a cluster of white sharks tearing it apart, limb by limb. What type of rage or evil can overcome nature, if these sharks are even natural anymore for these frigid waters of the North Atlantic? Limbs and half a face, more like half a skull missing, and it still laughs. It still comes towards me as I watch on in absolute shock and fright. Until it is finally pulled under water to not return to the surface. Several sharks still swarm around my boat, but the pirate doesn't resurface, even though I can still hear it laughing underwater somehow.

Or is it the rest of the demon pirates that are laughing as the current creates further distance between me and the sinking Sea Hellion? The only visible light is the burning phantom ship and each of the dead pirates on board. It even engulfed Scotty and Yellow Jack in flames, but their noose never falters to drop them down on the deck. I drift further and further away into the storm, leaving a trail of blood for the herd of sharks to follow, but the phantom ship, nor its occupants, make pursuit of me. They scurry about on the ropes to make their way off the Sea Hellion as more explosions from within the hull set the ship's remains above water on fire. As they get closer to their own ship, the individual flames on themselves return brighter again. The Sea Hellion sinks down fast as soon as the phantom ship releases its ropes until the Sea Hellion is no more. For the sea has claimed her as her own now too. All that remains are me on my sad attempt at a life raft and the ship of burning sails.

I stare at these living corpses of pirates as I drift away with the currents and the stormy seas. They stare back at me while still engulfed in flames that can only be fueled by a hatred and wickedness that their ship gives them. The last glimpse of light beyond the lightning is those red eyes that glow brighter than the ship and the crew of the dead. The phantom ship's captain appears to be more evil and vile than the rest. Then the burning ship fades away, back into a darkness from hence it came as I am left alone to wander in the frigid waters. My ship and fellow seamen are gone. I am all that remains, but for how long, I do not know. Life is bleeding out of my foot faster than I can control. Everything is just dark and cold as I am tossed around in this vicious sea of the damned.

Chapter 21 - The Phantom Ship

No one is coming for me. There is no one out there as I look around. I am alone on the deepest level possible. Alone in the vast horrid emptiness of the ocean that is the truest unknown left to man. The storm has subsided after a night of being tossed around on my upside-down boat. All that remains are the gray skies that seem to have no horizon with the gray waters all around me. There is no sun through the overcast to even see the direction of the currents. My only means of survival is a small fillet knife. No water and I can't remember my last meal when I touch my chapped lips.

Even though the daunting storms and waves have calmed, the freezing cold shrouded by the fog still remains. Even the sharks are looming as blood from my foot and shredded calf muscle slowly drips off into the sea. It's as if they are waiting for me to end or commit myself into the sea, despite my pant leg wrapped around my thigh to slow the bleeding. Whenever my eyes seem to close, they nudge the bottom of the boat for a test. Or maybe to remind me that they are still there and waiting for me. One solid bite, and this dinghy would sink in minutes, then they would finally have their feast, because I have no energy or strength to swim away. There is nowhere to swim to.

Dehydrated and freezing now. My lips are so chapped it feels like they scratch my tongue whenever I lick them for moisture. I'll just wait in the cold, waiting for my turn. Waiting for the end and think of something better in the meantime. I think of her and what she may have had to say in that last phone call. I never even checked the voicemail before I threw it down on the beach to break it into several pieces. Maybe I should have called her back. I try to think of her in a way that helps me stay warm while I remain curled up on the boat, but it's hard when the intrusive thoughts come in. The thoughts that maybe I was wrong in all of that somehow. The thought of maybe I pushed her away to fall into someone else's arms. The thought that she was right to leave me in the manner she did.

Guilt and regret on my part are all I can comprehend when thinking of her, even though she lied to me. My mother liked her the few times they met. But she didn't care to go to my mother's funeral. Maybe the times she met my mother were all just a show for her. A show that maybe I fell for too. Was any of it ever real? Was any of it ever real for her? Is any of the last several days real for me? This pathetic sulking may kill me faster than the elements out here, only in just wanting it all to end sooner. But what I wonder is not knowing if my name will at least be on that same memorial where this all started, as another lowly fisherman lost to the sea.

Last night's cannon fire and guns blazin' left my ears ringing something fierce. I hold my beanie down over my ears to try to blotch it out and help with the cold at the same time. But it's no use. The sound of a broken violin plays and echoes out in the fog. She's still out there, only looming in the fog, drifting and awaiting my demise, so I may join the rest of my crew mates. The phantom ship still drifts and roams all around me in the mists, it seems. What is she waiting for? What are these malicious sharks waiting for? This sense of pending end must be a torture for some unknown wrongdoing, only to be greeted with more cruelty afterwards. How and when will this end out here?

My silent pleads derived from a guilt I didn't know I carry are abruptly answered when I shudder from the splash of a tail fin sending icy saltwater at me. My body aches as I get up on my knees and prepare for the worst. There must be half a dozen shark fins floating around, going into a frenzy by the smell of my blood trickling off the side of the boat. Not to mention how many I may not see still under the water. But to my surprise, or blurred vision, they seem to swim away. None of them are trying to bite at the boat. Some of the dorsal fins are above water, but they are all moving away from me in the same direction. The sound of the broken violin draws close, and I turn around to see what the sharks are swimming away from. The phantom ship quietly approaches me out of the fog. Sails tucked up on the masts and every inch is charred black from the mysterious fire that it was in last night when attacking us.

    It's a beast of a ship, burned to a crisp and smoking, but still silently glides over the calm waters. I don't even have the energy to be saddened anymore. If I were to try an elaborate escape and make a swim for it, I might be too tempted to just sink and drown. I just sit and watch as this sea faring hearse draws near me before coming to a stop. I drop off my knees and shiver from the cold and fear, waiting for one of its many burning demon pirates to look over the side with a pistol in hand to take a shot at me. But there's nothing but quiet. Even the broken and screeching violin stops playing as the ship comes to a stop right next to me. Maybe they have a cannon I can't see aimed at me. Maybe they would prefer to slice me open to spew the last of my insides into the ocean. What are they waiting for? They know I can't escape from this, so why keep waiting anymore?

"The hell with this..." I tuck my fillet knife into my waist before I purposely fall over the side of the boat. The water takes my breath away as I attempt to swim away. My leg and the bite wounds at my feet sting for a moment, then resort to going numb again from the cold. I make it a few feet away from my boat and my thighs cramp up on me. My hands and arms are numb. Water fills my lungs, before I am dragged to the surface by something. A net has surrounded me and is pulling me towards the ship. I cough and hack out the sea water, some through my mouth and the rest out my nose. I reach through the net and try to hold on to my tiny dinghy boat, but my grip is too weak to use it as a means to weigh myself down. They are all pulling me up the side of the ship as I bounce around inside the net against the dark wood. They continue to drag me up, and I ready my fillet knife. That's when I see a name on the side of the ship through the net. She is the Chaleur.

On the deck and still tangled in the net, I drop like a sack of rocks, lifeless and cold. But there is no one or nothing there that dragged me up the side of the ship. Every being on board is just a charred up skeletal remains. I don't even know how I got up here if nobody, dead or living, pulled me up here. I squirm out of the net but am still too weak to stand up. Especially with a torn-up calf and foot. I look up and see what remains of Yellow Jack and Scotty. Scotty still has that sword stuck in his torso, and Yellow Jack only has a few stitches of his jacket left on him. Either way, they are also burned to a crisp while left hanging on the noose from the top sails. Everything that was dead just seems more dead now. Every corpse that lies on the deck, some look familiar, some don't, is just lying around lifeless and burned to the bones. I stand up, limping and keep weight off my injured leg, and see remains near me. It has a bullet hole through the side of his skull. I know it's Skipper Walsh as I slowly step over him and see those familiar jailhouse tattoos on his hands. There's just so many of them, all lying around dead on the cold damp ship that has been burned up as much as the rest of them. Some have swords drawn, and some with pistols in hand.

But there is one that sits upright. Still blackened from the flames and a mere resemblance of a skeletal remains in scorched clothing. I walk closer and see it is missing most of a leg. It slowly turns its head out to sea and raises a violin and bow up to its shoulder. He wears the same hat I do. He has the same mutilated leg as I do. I hear bones creak and crack as it raises the violin bow to play that same scratchy tune I have heard on the radio. It just looks out to sea, not phased be me standing near it as if I'm not even here. Each movement it makes, despite being dead, still appears painful for it. I don't see how this living corpse could ever play a proper tune. I don't want to accept the idea that this is supposed to be me somehow. I keep my knife pointed at it, but it doesn't even acknowledge me. Its chest has clothes seared to it. It's hands have my same bandages from my rope burns trying to save Diesel. It just sits there and plays that broken tune. I limp around on the deck, smoking and smelling of burnt oat wood, trying to avoid stepping on any of them. The small fires that still remain in various places of the ship are the first warmth I have felt in what feels like forever now. How many has this ship claimed and has it already claimed me? I just don't know it yet.

A set of doors forcefully open near the back of the ship and I stumble on another scorched body of bones.

A dark whisper comes across the deck in a raspy voice, "Dine with the damned…"

The same voice says it multiple times, but the whispers come from all directions. I look down and see that the corpse's lips move in unison as the whispers continue.

"Dine with the damned…"

I don't know what is drawing me closer to the rear of the ship, but I look back at the dead violinist that looks like me and he has lowered his bow. He just stares with that face of charred up bone and death. Its teeth are bare to give me a smile at first glance, but I know it's just the seared remains of its mouth and jaw.

"Dine with the damned…" whispering again and again as I walk into the lowly lit room shrouded in darkness. Only a single candle is lit on a table. Showing a cluster of dusty maps, a spoiled plate of food, and navigation tools. A heavy cough overcomes me, and I lean over to dry heave from the smell of rotting fester. I limp into the room further and can see the ocean through the ship's rear windows. My cough won't back down and I accidentally put all my weight on the shredded foot, just to drop down to my knees. I try to hold myself from a fall, but a single stool mysteriously slides in front of me to brace my fall as the doors behind me slowly close me in. I try to reach for the doors to keep them from closing, but everything on this phantom ship appears to be at a tilt. My bearings are gone from exhaustion, or maybe I am still in a hellish nightmare that just won't end.

The deck was warm from the recent flames, but this room is colder than the sea I was lost in. I look all around the room as my eyes adjust, then I see those red eyes have been watching me all along. Far enough away from the single candlelight on the table, but close enough to see the silhouette of a man. This is death's quarters. This is the captain's cabin. I stare back at the low glaring red eyes of a captain that commands a ghost ship. He, or maybe it, has the same charred and burnt face as the rest of them. The demon pirate commander stands up from behind the table and the cold hits deeper than I ever felt before.

"Every day, I die… Every day," comes a rasping voice from the room.

It's still too dark for a full depiction of its face or body. It's an imposing figure, but walks like a living nobleman, as it looks out the back window of the cabin. His stance strays away from the light overcast through the windows, as if the light of day burdens him.

"I see my beasts have kept you company in these trying days for you, young Isaac. Defiant to the very end…"

Jesus… This thing speaks. This monster speaks to me and knows my name. It holds its arms behind its back as it gazes out the window.

"A healer that cannot heal himself. Tell me, why do you look for a means to mend yourself out here? Just look out at her. Listen to her whisper to us, both the living and the dead."

Its voice is almost theatrical as it, or he, points out the window with an outstretched limb. That's when I see a hand, only mere bones and hanging skin. He speaks to me somehow, but I can't see a mouth moving.

"I've deliberated for many years now, how something so beautiful can be so cruel."

The dead thing turns around and walks back to the chair behind the table. He leans over and I see its attire and black coat, dingy and filled with rips and burns, stitched back together on multiple occasions. It sits back down into the chair, tired and beaten down, barely visible in the candlelight.

"Did you hear her? Can you hear her whisper? Do you know what she said to me?"

I just listen intently with confusion and horror as I have a conversation with a ghost. It just looks down at the maps on the table, almost sad somehow. "I can't hear her anymore. She used to whisper to me. But now I can't hear her… Do you know what she said to me before it all went dark? I took her husband. Then I took her innocence, and then… Then I took her life. A young bride to be ravaged and ended. A life bled out, cut open at her own throat well before her own time. Now the whispering widow of the sea…"

I can't stop shaking in this chair. No means to run and no words to say.

"I remember what she said." Its eyes glow a brighter red. "For as long as this world is, may you burn in the bay."

It quickly stands up and retrieves the large round hat from a stand near his side of the table, putting it on and towering over me. As if the table has closed the distance between us on its own, somehow.

"Heed my words within my forever dying voice, boy. Lest I ever see you set sail again with the vile and the corrupt, I'll see to it that you too dine with the damned so that they will also make you eaters of men."

It reaches for a sword, long and curved, that was hanging in a sheath on the backside of the chair. The captain walks to the front of his table, pointing the sword at me. I shudder in place as that blade comes close. It moves the sword with extreme precision and lifts my chin with its tip. I just keep my eyes closed not to look at it. Not to look at the dead thing that has come for me.

"Feast your eyes…"

I just shake my head.

"NOW!!!" and he cuts my chin with the tip of his sword.

I open my eyes and see torture. I see unholiness of the darkest kind in those burning red eyes. I see souls crushed by their own demise.

The sword stays trained on my chin and the captain scrubs it around my face. "Defy me on this, boy, and I promise your burning death with the rest of us, on a deck of brimstone, under sails of fire, will never end."

The captain backs his sword away from my face slightly and points it down at my shaking hands.

"I do so love the chase…" It points the sword towards my hands and pricks at my fingers until I open them and show my rope burned palms.

"But this chase was not meant for you."

The captain points the sword down at my palms and a small metal chain slides all the way down the blade into my hand. I look down at the chain and it's a necklace. My necklace. My mother's St. Peter. I look back up as he continues to walk away and look out the back of his ship. The unreal has become real and even demons have a place for sorrow and pain. He still stands as a tall nobleman and watches the foggy sea out the window of his cabin.

He turns his head, and I can hear bones cracking as he speaks over his shoulder, "The seas have claimed enough for herself on this day. Go now… Young Isaac. Best ye pray that we never meet again…"

I grip my St. Peter and stand from the stool with wobbly legs, trying to keep my weight off the one bleeding foot. This whole time I have said nothing, but this ghost has said everything I needed to hear. The candle begins to burn brighter. Even the old maps on his table smolder with smoke, yet the captain still remains turned away from me. The doorknob to the captain's quarters is burning hot to the touch. I open the door, but not without one last look at him. One last look at a ghost that has been orchestrating the passing of the Sea Hellion and her crew for the last several days. And he is now beginning to smolder in flames coming from up under his large black jacket. Despite being on fire, he straightens his tarnished hat and continues to look out at the sea. The thought passes over me, wondering if those dark gray waters were also, like me, his first true love at some point long ago.

I turn away and head out to the deck with a painful limp to see it is all going up in flames again. The sails have been lowered and engulfed in a burning blaze that stings the eyes. The crew, however, also beginning to go up in flames, stand by the outside of the door, lined up shoulder to shoulder on each side. They all snarl and look at me in contempt and a hatred that strikes the soul with daggers. None of them speak like the captain did. They just growl and grind their teeth at me, undeniably tempted to bite my heart out from my chest. They snap and reach for me, but none of them touch me as they are slowly engulfed in flames more and more with each step of my gimpy leg. Even the two left on a noose above, Scotty with a sword in his stomach and Yellow Jack, look down at me with such contempt that I can no more than glance at them as they twist and jerk their bodies around, but their heads do not move with them. They only stare down at me still. Any of them with a sword or pistol has it in hand, but none of them point their weapon at me. None of them have any concern that their ship is going a blaze again.

A demon crawls around on the deck in a struggle, reaching for his multiple charred body parts that have been severed from him. He holds one severed limb that's a hand with the arm that has been chopped away from his body. It stops in its struggle to collect his own body parts and just stares at me as I walk by. The deck boss of the Sea Hellion has found his torment on the phantom ship as well. At the side of the ship where I was dragged onboard, the ghostly singed Skipper Walsh readies a noose for me. He looks down at the small dinghy boat that has been tied off on the side of the ship and I see it has been turned over to normal. He turns back to look at me and the flames flutter out of the bullet hole in the side of his head. His mustache is barely holding on to his severed, charring lips. He just stares at me, confused and furious as to why this fate has befallen on him. He hands the noose over to me and I hook my arm through it to be lowered down to my tiny raft.

The broken violinist begins to hop around on one foot again, returning to his awful screeching tune that the rest attend to their work with. But there are no smiles, no laughter and bickering among men, only biting and gnashing of teeth at each other. Like I did with the captain in his quarters, I look back at all of them one last time. Most have begun to ignore me and carryout with their duties aboard a burning ship. They tighten down the ropes for the sails that are on fire. They raise anchors, red hot with heat. They prepare to set sail on a sea of torment for the rest of their days. To set sail and remain as black as their hearts were when they were among the living. Skipper Walsh just looks at me, no longer recognizing me, and lowers me down as if it were one of his known duties to see me off. He looks down at me from the side of the ship and I drop into the dinghy boat with no paddle. He unties the rope and throws it down at me.

I watch in horror as the blaze engulfs the ship that has claimed many and drifts away.

A ship that is full of the damned from many generations of the vile and greedy.

The sea fairing hearse with sails of fire returns to the fog that conceals it from its prey.

A fog that can only be derived in the cold from the gasping breaths of tortured souls.

Chapter 22 - Out of the Fog

Only a fever can make you feel so cold and so hot at the same time. I loosen up the wraps on my leg to try to keep circulation flowing to the wounds, but the feeling in my foot doesn't return. Only tingling with pins and needles. The shark bite to my calf has turned to a festering heap of bile and I can see fragments of bones in pieces in my foot. It won't be much longer now, but at least the storm has subsided. The waters are calm and blue for the first time since this all began. Not just a hazy blue from an overcast of the coming winter season, it is a true deep blue. It's a pleasant sight, but I barely have enough energy to sit up and appreciate it. There are no more sharks nudging at the boat, no more phantom ship lurking, nor a storm tossing me around in the fog. There is only me out here with a dwindling hope while my cold shivers grow deeper by the hour. I don't even know how long I keep my eyes closed in the sunlight. Could be for a few minutes or for hours at a time. Eventually, I may close my eyes and I won't wake back up. Even if I am found, how would I tell anybody what happened out here?

My dreams from a fever induced sleep are vivid and brief. I dream of being back home running around with kids on the shoreline. I dream of dancing around with other drunk fishermen at my mother's pub. I dream of my fiancé and how she left me. I dream of the struggles, good and bad, on the fishing boat with that rambunctious crew that I grew to work with. I dream of pirates holding me at the tip of a sword and wrapping a noose around my neck. I hear things in my dreams too.

I hear the dead pirates grunting and growling. I hear the storm waves crashing. I hear the music that we fished with. I hear it all in my dreams. But I don't remember hearing the sounds I hear now, because they are different. A low rumble at first, but it grows stronger and louder. I can only assume the storm has spit me out just to swallow me up again, but it doesn't sound like that monstrous storm returning from the distance. I can't remember if it's night or day, but the sun seems brighter than normal. I reach up at it to cover the blindness with my hand. I crawl my way up to the front of the boat to tuck my head up under one of the side walls to get away from the light. The light gets brighter and brighter, even with trying to block it with my hand.

That's not a normal light. That's a furious grumble of something heinous returning for me again. The sounds of those pirates grunting and growling at me, blasting into my ears. This is not the end, because I'm not ready. I hold my St. Peter tight with one shivering hand and pull out the fillet knife in the other. With my eyes closed in the blinding lights, I wave it around with the last bit of adrenaline I can gather. But it's not enough. One of them grabs my hand in the struggle while slinging my knife around at them, splashing cold sea water into the boat.

An unfamiliar voice yells over the rumble, "He's alive!"

A strong hand holds my wrist out to yank the knife from my weakened grip. Water splashes over my lips and I spit it out, thinking its seawater.

"It's water! Drink slowly!" The same voice yells over the roaring noise around us.

Someone is holding my head up to drink from a water bottle. The powerful light shining on my face is coming from above in the night sky. Everything is a blur, and I cough with each sip of water.

"Lower the basket! He's in bad shape!"

The spotlight moves away, and I see a face covered in goggles and swim gear. I reach out to touch it and the stranger just looks at me. He raises his goggles off his eyes as I touch his face. He just looks at me as I question if this is real or not while touching his face covered in dive gear. The rumble spins on all around, but it's not just a noise. It's a helicopter.

I look at him again as he lowers his goggles back on. Another cold splash as he jumps into the water to swim towards a cable attached to a basket that has already been lowered near the boat. He comes back to the side with the cable in hand.

"Can you move at all!?!?"

I don't know how to answer. I just point down at my leg. At a closer look, he sees me scratching at my tourniquet. He leans in closer to yell into my ear over the sound of the helicopter above.

"You're safe now! But I gotta put you in the water for just a little bit so I can get you in the basket! If you have any strength left, you need to use it now so we can lift you outta here! Ok?!" yelling over the helicopter above.

I give him the thumbs up and shake my head. I slowly lift myself up and he helps me roll over into the frigid waters. I scream in pain when the cold hits me, but notice my hands are empty. There's no knife or St. Peter in hand. I try to reach for the boat, but I don't have any strength left. He does most of the work, swimming my limp frozen body over to the basket. All I can do is point to the boat, but my throat is too dry to tell him to go back. He drops me upright into the rescue basket and my head falls back limp. He crosses my arms over my chest as he straps me down.

"Hold the lift!" he says, while giving a hand signal to the pilot above us in the helicopter.

He swims back to the boat before it drifts away and reaches inside. He swims back against the currents as if he belongs on an Olympic swim team. Only a Coast Guard rescue diver can swim like that. He opens one of my hands crossed over my chest and shows me that he went back for my St. Peter. He puts it into my palm and closes my fist with significance before placing my hand back over my chest.

"Raise the lift!!!" he yells, as he gives more hand signals to the helicopter above.

I am brought up out of the water and into the cold air. The winds from the helicopter send more shivers all over me. I'm greeted with a face mask pumping life into me and a cluster of blankets covering me as they drag me out of the basket. They try to move my hands, but my arms have cramped in place.

A needle goes into my arm and they shine more pen lights in my eyes. A sting travels up my leg as they pour alcohol on my injured leg. I flinch and jerk around from the pain, but several of them hold me down. Whatever was in that needle or whatever they keep holding up to my nose brings me back to life in an instant. My eyes are clear, and I see one of them placing a set of headphones over my ears.

"Can you hear me? Can you hear my voice?" One of them asks through the headphones.

He holds me upright and I shake my head yes.

"Are there any other survivors with you?"

I breathe in through the oxygen mask and shake my head no. I look around the helicopter and see a few more of my rescuers. One of them stays at the edge of the doors, helping the diver get loaded back in. The medic lifts off my mask to have me drink water through a straw, then lowers it back down over my face. He turns to shake his head no at the other crewmembers on board. Another medic looks over my leg and is attempting to clean it up.

Several more needles go in, but he just wraps my leg up. He yells something at the pilot while shaking his head no. The chopper maneuvers around faster once the rescue diver is back on board. I see my tiny boat start to get smaller and smaller as we glide away in the air.

"What ship were you on?" One of them asks through the headphones.

I lift the mask briefly. "Sea Hellion."

He shakes his head yes as he talks to the other crewmembers.

"He's with the other American. The big Indian man we scooped up the other day." He looks back at me. "How many were on your ship?"

I have to think in my head. My vision may have come back, but everything seems surreal to me right now. I raise my hands and try to hold up seven fingers. He just shakes his head at me and goes up to sit next to the pilot. They all keep working on me, mainly my leg.

"Don't... Don't let them take my leg," I plead as they lean me back down to lie flat. "Don't let them take..." As I grab the medic's hand. He just looks at me. He doesn't agree or say anything back, he just looks at me in disappointment.

The rescue diver comes over to divert my attention. "Look at me, kid," he says through the headphones. "Just talk to me through the headphones. Save your energy and let them do their part, alright?"

"How'd you find me?"

He looks over at the pilot that turns around and gives him a head nod to answer my question. "Your charter already had the US Coast Guard on alert when they hadn't heard from you guys for a few days during the storm. The US called us to relay the same thing. Earlier today we got a radio distress call from a smaller fishing boat in the Gulf that they spotted a ship in the distance that was on fire. We thought that it was you guys on the Sea Hellion, so we came right out."

"The Gulf? You're not American?" I ask him.

He just shakes his head no with a smile. "You Yanks must have let the storm blow you in all the way from the Grand Banks. Only a crazy American would be trawling the banks this time of year. You're in Canadian waters. The Gulf of St. Lawrence between Nova Scotia and Newfoundland there, kid," as he pats my chest to humor me.

"We were that close…"

He just shakes his head yes again, with that same smile. But his smile fades quickly when he sees my head go down in tears and sadness. "We were that close…"

There's only so much support he can give as the diver that pulled me from the icy waters. So, he resorts to, "It's over, kid. You're safe now, aye. Just try to relax."

He goes to turn away from me back to his seat near the door, "Wait," as I grab him. He turns back around. "They said there was another?"

"Right, big Indian guy. Doesn't speak a word of English or French. Found him clinging to life in the cold seas on a bunch of fishing buoys. Guessing him and all that gear was blown off your ship in the storm. He was with your crew, right?"

I shake my head yes and lay my head back down. He taps my chest again for good measure before he goes to his seat. I look out the other side of the chopper, still crying from learning just how close we are to the land that I can now see in the distance, but glad that I'm not the only one that has survived this nightmare.

The pain in my leg lets me know that I'm not dreaming, even though the lack of energy makes my eyes want to close. I just want to see the land come closer to me before I drift off again. I just want to feel the ground under my two feet again.

Because we were that close to it all along.

We were all just that damn close…

Chapter 23 - Going Ahab

An ambulance ride and moving from different stretchers to a bed leaves a new blur to comprehend as I come in and out of reality. Everything, again, feels surreal now that the floors and decks are not constantly shifting with waters and winds. Reporters and camera flashes flood the outside of the hospital. Law enforcement and Canadian Coast Guard are demanding to see me, but the doctors and nurses waste no time in dealing with them and shoo them away. Hospital guards barricade doors to keep their unwanted quests out. All I see roaming around me, as I drift in and out, are nurses and doctors.

"He's got a serious fever, let's get him cooled down," one says.

"It's just too far gone," says another.

Another mask over my face and lights are shining all around in my eyes. I don't want to fall asleep again. I need to walk on land just for the sake of knowing this isn't a dream. I grab the arm of the first person walking by me. It's a female nurse with a typical hospital mask.

"What's happening?" I lower the oxygen mask off to talk.

She just stares at me with those big green eyes, hesitant about what to say. "We gotta perform a surgery on your leg. We gotta put you under, though. You're gonna be just fine." She puts the mask back over me. "Count back from five for me, ok..."

I don't even make it to five before my eyes close. Whatever they were doing to fix my leg and foot from the shark attack, I could have just fallen asleep on my own from fever and exhaustion so they could do what they needed to do with no fight from me. Everything is dark and peaceful, but it all seems to go by so fast when put under for surgery.

When I wake up, I discover that they put me in a damn room with a window overlooking the ocean bay. I turn my head to see the storm clouds in the distance. Familiar storm clouds with an endless supply of lightning. The beeps and whirs from all the medical equipment attached to me are faint, but I find the help button to bring a nurse in. *Green eyes* returns, and I recognize her right away.

"How do you feel, sir?" she asks.

I point out the window, "How long has that storm been brewing?"

She looks out the window. "That's the same one from the last few days. It just hasn't hit land fall yet. They said you were out there in it and your ship went down. You're the luckiest guy I know right now, especially to have survived that." She lifts my blankets to help me sit up. But there are no fresh bandages on my leg, because my leg isn't even there. They took my leg just below the knee. She sees that I notice my missing leg for the first time and tries to comfort me.

"They really tried, sir. I'm so sorry, but it was just so far gone."

"You were in there with them when they took it?" She just shakes her head yes. "I don't think this is a matter of being lucky then, is it?"

She sits me up on the bed, ignoring what I just said, and looks over all the tubes and medical equipment. I raise my hand as she looks at the thermometer. "Thank you for your help. I didn't..." She pauses in her efforts to look right back at me. "I didn't mean that against you, or anything like that. But I thank you... The doctor too. All of you."

"It's ok. I'm sure it's a lot to take in right now. This is a big change for you, but you're alive and safe now."

"Can we just keep it covered with the blanket for a while longer after you're done?" I ask.

"Of course."

She finishes her duties and does as I ask. She even pulls out additional blankets. I just stare out the window, looking at the storm I survived. It would be easy to sit here and wonder why me? Why couldn't we make it just a little further to get to land already being in Canadian waters? Why was I spared in all this, just to be left mutilated?

I look down at the stand next to my bed and see the note for Diesel's beloved Boo. The paper is now tarnished and torn apart from saltwater exposure. Next to it is my St. Peter. Then I am reminded everything must have happened for a reason. Everything prior to all the nightmarish events and chaos was more than just a tolerable effort. Being out there was enjoyable and had meaning before it all went to hell.

"Shall I go get him?" she asks, breaking me from my trance.

"What?"

"Your friend… The other survivor. Doesn't talk much, but he's alive and well. I discharged him a few days ago, then he came right back as soon as word got out there was another survivor. He's been waiting for you."

"How long have I been out?"

"You've been in and out of it the last few days. The guards ran off all the reporters and lawyers trying to get in to see you. But he's the only one that stayed in the waiting area. I don't think the guards tried to send him away, actually."

I start to smile and chuckle under my breath. "I think I know why that is, but why don't you tell me why the guards wouldn't approach him?"

Her eyes light up with my sense of humor and she smiles. "Oh, he scares the crap out of them. He looks mean, but he was nice to me when I was working with him. Both of you guys are pretty lucky."

I just smile and shake my head. "Yeah... He is pretty brutish looking."

She just stands between the bed and the window, smiling from ear to ear without saying anything. "What is it?" I ask, while she still stands there.

"You have a nice smile. It's good to smile after what you've been through, Isaac. That's what your name means."

I just look back at her, puzzled.

"Isaac, son of Abraham. Isaac means joyous or joyful. So... it's good to see you smile now that you're awake."

I reach over for my St. Peter and hold it in my hand. "Right... I forget about that." I smile back at her, "Send him in please."

Green eyes steps out and comes back with him in a hurry. I can see his massive shadow in the hallway from the doorway she left open. This hospital must not be very big. Of course, my room does has a clear view of the approaching storm. Comanche walks in, strong and tall with half a smile. His hair is back in a ponytail to show all of his face tattoos. I'm sure he did that on purpose to scare all the people and nurses. He sees me and raises his fists in celebration.

"And my Isaac lives to fish another day," he says.

"You too Comanche," as I grab and shake his hand.

The same nurse grabs him a chair from the hallway to bring in. She quickly places it next to the bed for him to have a seat between me and the window. He also notices the storm approaching the bay from the ocean.

The nurse smiles again. "Just buzz if you two need anything, ok?"

I shake my head while Comanche and I both watch the show from behind as she walks out the door.

Comanche points her out as soon as the door closes, "Pretty nurse..."

"Now Comanche, don't forget what you told me... *Women*..."

He smiles and agrees, "Yes...*Women*."

"It's good to see ya, big guy, but how in the hell did you survive that one?"

He stands up with excitement. I haven't seen him with such enthusiasm since we were hauling in nets filled with fish. "First, I swim many miles. Then sharks come for me." He shows me his left hand, now missing its pinky and ring fingers. "I fight sharks with my own teeth and blade." He pulls out that familiar bowie knife from when we first met and swishes it around, as if still fighting sharks, grunting and growling with his tongue out.

I smile at his possible exaggeration. Until it hits me, "Wait... They said they found you clinging to life with a buoy in the middle of the ocean, half frozen?"

He puts his knife away and sits back down, "Yes... This is true, but after many miles of swim and many a dead shark."

"For some reason that I cannot place at the moment, I find everything you just said completely believable." But he doesn't seem to catch my sarcasm. "But I'm afraid I have you beat, ol' buddy." I lift up my blanket to reveal my missing leg.

He gasps at first. It saddens him to see me mutilated like this, but a man of few words like him only says what needs to be said and nothing more. "Nah!" He raises his hands in a scoff. "We get you new leg. New leg like the Moby Dick," he says.

"Moby Dick was the whale in the story, Comanche..." He just stares back at me with a blank look. "Moby Dick, ya know, was the whale. Captain Ahab was, like... Well... Never mind... I forget that you probably don't read that much, do you?" He just looks at me with that same blank stare and then commits to smiling again.

I laugh lightly as he sits there with a smile. He moves closer to the bed and we both look out the window to see the approaching storm.

He looks back at me and says, "I hear my Sedna still calling for us, young Isaac. Did you find what it is that you seek?"

"I don't know what I was looking for out there, Comanche."

"Yes you do…"

"And what is that?" I ask, while covering up my leg with the blanket again.

"Purpose, my friend." He points out the window.

"Right…" I look out the window with him. "I guess I just had to get lost to find it first. Yeah?"

He shakes his head yes, "She still calls for you. My Sedna gives life to all…"

"And fishing is life," I say, finishing his statement for him.

He shakes his head yes.

Despite all that has happened, I no longer feel troubled. Still missing a leg yet revived somehow. "Well, Comanche… The nurse already said there were lawyers outside waiting to talk to me." He just shakes his head yes as I keep him in mild suspense. He leans in closer to listen intently. "They'll want to know what happened and offer compensation that they see fit. But they don't want the public to know what *really* happened out there. So… They can either pay for a limb that won't grow with a lifetime of medical needs to go with. Or…" He just leans in closer. "Or we lease our own ship from the charter for bottom dollar cost to us."

His interest grows instantly. "Skipper your own boat?" he asks with eagerness.

"Gonna need a crew and a trusty first mate with some experience to help me out at first, 'cause I've never been behind the wheel of a boat like that. But how hard could it be to catch a bunch of damn fish?"

He reaches out his hand to shake mine again while saying, "Where you go, I follow now… My friend. For as long as this world is."

"Sir," the green-eyed nurse walked in at some point while we were talking. "We keep getting the same lady calling the hospital. She says she's your fiancé."

Comanche lets go of my hand, but still keen of my grand plan.

"Umm… Right… If you could, just write her number down and the country code and I will call her back in a few minutes."

She shakes her head yes and walks out again.

Comanche stands up from the chair to walk out, "I shall take my leave, Isaac. Heal fast and we go fishing again, yes?"

I agree with a head nod. "Wait, did you see it? The ship that took us down. I mean... What do we tell them about our friends that died out there? They're gonna have so many questions. There's just so much that happened and the things we saw..."

He leans in again, standing over me. "We say nothing." I look at him with my own blank stare in confusion this time. He continues on, "We tell them nothing, Isaac. They don't understand. The dead blue sea came for them. Sad, but whispering widow called for them. The dead blue sea called for them. She almost got us too. She came from black mists and took them all back. It brought with it sails of fire and a fury of the sea. To bring all those she calls for back into the darkness from where it came... Go back to her," as he points out the window.

"Answer the call of Sedna. Answer the call for life, not the dead blue sea's. There're many lost souls out there. She needs no more." He stands back up straight and shakes my hand again. "You saw what needed to be seen. Now fishermen, we will remain, my friend."

I can always count on Comanche, that in everything he says it is always inarguable. He lets go of my hand again and walks out. He leaves as mysteriously as he entered. He walks with his head held high. I will admit, I would do the same if I had both legs at the moment. His massive presence startles the cluster of nurses outside the door. Of course, he would also take advantage of that without hesitation.

"We go fishing!!!" He yells at several of them with excitement as he walks by waving his arms around. One nurse gets so startled by him, she yelps in fear and drops her tray of medical supplies she was walking around with. The door to my room closes behind him as he walks away down the hallway he came from and the nurses commit to picking up their supplies. Scoffing and cursing him as he walks away with a grin on his face.

Green eyes quickly returns with what I asked, and I sit up on the edge of my bed to reach for the phone. One leg hangs over, and the other does not. The nurse stays for a second, but I give her the nod that quietly asks for some privacy again.

I dial the number she gave me on a small piece of paper and the phone rings. My heart sinks in my chest when I hear her voice say, *"I'm sorry, but I'm not available right now. Please leave a message after the beep…"*

It's the first time I've heard her voice in weeks, but it is just a voice with no meaning to me now. She probably didn't answer from not recognizing an odd out-of-country number. But she WILL recognize my words and my voice when she hears them both. I wait to hear the phone dial beep to say what I now know needs to be said to end this chapter.

"Whatever you had to say in your last voicemail before I came out here will never matter to me, because I never really mattered to you. You lied to me. You lied to me over and over again, but that doesn't matter anymore. Life has now and will always move on without you, but I know you can never say the same thing. You may think you found something better, but it won't last being built on lies.

I tried to warn you that there were so many like you, but you turned out just like the rest of them. I've seen them run away to care for only themselves when things got hard and I told you not to be like them, but you didn't listen to me. I don't care to know you or remember you ever again. Some things are worth the chase, but you are not. You never were. I'm hanging up now and you're not worth my goodbye. Because you can't hurt me anymore… No one can."

I hang up the phone before the voicemail times out. Then I take it a step further and unplug the landline cord out from the back of the phone so I can heal in peace now.

I look out the window to see her and how a normal person would hold so much contempt for the ocean in my position. But I do not.

When I see a glimpse of lightning from that storm that rages over her through the window, I am somehow set as ease. The skies have turned her even more gray and colder with the nearing winter season. Again, I stare in awe before my first true love as she whispers to all those nearby willing to listen. She remains a true temptress in every sense that can claim the lowly.

With her is a place to find passion and cruelty.
She covets and hates, loves and lives with many.
But I remain at her summoning when she calls.
And I shall return to her time and time again.
Because nothing else makes sense anymore.
For she is the deadliest type of beautiful to me.
She is the sea…

The Fisherman's Prayer

God Grant that I may live to fish
until my dying day,
and when it comes to my last cast,
I then most humbly pray,
When in the Lord's safe landing net,
I'm peacefully asleep,
That in His mercy I be judged
as good enough to keep.

(-original Author unknown-)

About the Author

Corey Phillips was born and raised in Newport, TN, and graduated from Cosby High School in 2007. He was Honorably Discharged from the Army in 2015 after serving two combat tours to Afghanistan. He now resides in Saltville, VA, with his wife and children and travels to various events throughout the region selling his books.

The Dead Blue Sea is Corey's third novel.